HOTELS OF NORTH AMERICA

ALSO BY RICK MOODY

FICTION

Garden State

The Ice Storm

The Ring of Brightest Angels Around Heaven

Purple America

Demonology

The Diviners

Right Livelihoods

The Four Fingers of Death

NONFICTION

Joyful Noise: The New Testament Revisited

(coeditor, with Darcey Steinke)

The Black Veil

On Celestial Music

HOTELS OF
NORTH AMERICA

A Novel

RICK MOODY

The author is grateful to Christine Elaine Torok for permission to reprint her Amazon.com review of Haribo Sugar-Free Teddy Bears.

First published in Great Britain in 2016 by Serpent's Tail,
an imprint of Profile Books Ltd
3 Holford Yard
Bevin Way
London
WC1X 9HD
www.serpentstail.com

First published in 2015 by Little, Brown and Company, New York

1 3 5 7 9 10 8 6 4 2

Designed by Marie Mundaca

Printed and bound in Great Britain by Clays, St Ives plc

A CIP record for this book can be obtained from the British Library

ISBN 978 1 78125 581 0
eISBN 978 1 78283 220 1

For Laurel and Hazel

HOTELS OF NORTH AMERICA

HOTELS OF NORTH AMERICA

The Collected Writings of
Reginald Edward Morse

Preface by Greenway Davies, Director, North American
Society of Hoteliers and Innkeepers

With an Afterword by Rick Moody

Preface

by Greenway Davies, Director, North American Society
of Hoteliers and Innkeepers

As I write these lines it's early spring in the Northeast, and Americans of every age and station are getting back into their cold, muddy, salt-befouled automobiles. They are lining up again at the airports, notwithstanding the humorless security protocols of the current air-traffic moment. The siren melody of spring break is calling to the college-age hedonists of America. And before long it will be Memorial Day, one of the heaviest travel weekends of the calendar year. We here in the New World are "on the move," going where the "weather suits our clothes," where we have business, where we have family, or where there is simply good old-fashioned entertainment.

With almost five million guest rooms in the greater United States, and another two hundred and forty thousand available in Canada, these hotels and motels are our residences, here in this part of the world, when we are away from home. Think of that motel by the side of the interstate at two in the morning when you've put in eleven or twelve hours driving your son's dormitory furniture back east, and the double lines on the road are starting to blur into four. That motel is there for you, like a friend outstretching

5

a hand. Think of that big sexy flamingo-pink Art Deco hotel on the beach in Miami that you stayed in during your first trip to the Florida coast, when you were amazed by the mashing up of Cuban intrigue, dance clubs, and beach culture. What a mark that hotel made on you. That hotel was where you danced until you aggravated your lumbago.

Where once we spent the weekend with family and friends, now we have some fifty thousand distinct hotel properties from which to choose. Think about it. Wherever exhaustion takes place, wherever a young couple wishes to pull over to dance the dance of new love, there's a hotel at the suitable price point. Hotels hilarious, anonymous, modest, opulent, strange. And how much finer is the welcome of that hotel or motel, how much more discreet and accepting is that hotel address, than the household of someone you barely knew in high school who has in the decades since fallen into some pretty unusual habits, including middle-of-the-night binge eating as you lie sleepless atop the uncomfortable foldout couch in the living room. Or, contrarily, how much better is that hotel than the apartment of some down-at-the-heel washerwoman who is now capable of taking into her "guest room" a few foreign nationals and sharing a percentage of her profits with an online front operation funded by Middle Eastern venture capitalists and their cronies.

Only a North American hotel can earnestly equip you with a mint on your pillow. Only a North American hotel has the fully outfitted minibar complete with selection of salty snack foods and popular sweets. Moreover, in today's fast-moving digital world, when you go to choose from our fifty thousand distinct hotel properties, you can have evaluations of the hotels and motels right at your fingertips with just a few clicks of your smartphone. These reviews, through which you might browse at this very moment, provide important criteria. We know that you often rely on ratings for your hotel choices and we appreciate that. And while we here at the North American Society of Hoteliers and Innkeepers think that each and every one of our thirty-two thousand dues-paying members are rolling out the welcome mat in a way that is designed to give you, our customer, exactly what you want, we recognize that you have strong feelings about where you are going to stay tonight, and it is our job to honor those feelings. When you write a review of our member establishments, you should do so without reservation, with joy in your heart and the kind of word choice that we associate with the romantic poets.

However, we here at NASHI recognize that there are times when no matter what we do, despite our best efforts—it's not often but it can happen—very occasionally we are going to let you down. Or we are going to misunderstand your wishes. And we realize that instead of trying to hide away these bad experiences somewhere you will never see them, in some Arctic Circle digital-storage facility, such that we never learn from our shortcomings, we might use your evaluations as part of an ambitious plan to *improve* hotel service in this country beyond its already significant level of achievement. We ought to listen to our critics and prize their sturdy unshakable opinions.

Accordingly, NASHI has conceived of this small, high-end run of books of various online reviews of lodging: the harsh, the laudatory, the fanciful, the elaborate, the joyful, and the melancholy. The inaugural volumes are off the press as we speak, including the hotel pet stories and the frothy poolside-party stories. We also have the already very popular anthology of hotel-related hauntings.

But we have gone even further. We think that whenever we find particular travel writers who are of unique and enduring value, we ought to commission a selection of their finest writings about hotels too. You may not always agree with these writers in our travel-writing series, but you will find something to make you laugh!

As you know, having laid your hands on this book on the coffee table or atop the desk or perhaps in the bedside drawer, right alongside the Scripture, our idea is to make these collectible volumes accessible to you right in your room, wherever you are lying down, talking on the phone, or watching the television, having kicked off the standard-issue paisley comforter, as it were, and eaten that chocolate mint on your pillow. Many more of these titles will become available in your favorite boutique hotels over the next twelve months. A few will be found exclusively in some of our finest five-star establishments. Consider these one-of-a-kind travel books our gift to you for spending your hard-earned income on hotel rooms and thereby providing, in an unprecedented show of consumer support, a livelihood for our hoteliers and their employees, many of whom are newly naturalized citizens of America and Canada, as well as a rich vein of revenue for states, provinces, and local municipalities. We thank you. Our belief is that your stay in our hotels is not an isolated, forgettable experience, a blip on the screen of twenty-first-century existence. Our belief is that your journey through the many dozens of hotels in which you have stayed is a second life of a sort, an additional life story, a place somewhere between your everyday, commonplace existence and a dream world where your every whim is catered to and your every appetite fulfilled.

The Collected Writings of Reginald Edward Morse, which you have before you here, is one such account. It is a heartwarming, funny-bone-tickling volume about the peaks and troughs of itinerant life. It's about rebirth and rehabilitation. (Or so my staff tells me; I haven't had time to read the whole series yet! Which means I need a vacation!) It is also, they say, not strictly chronological but is being presented in the same manner in which it was composed, which is to say, most impulsively, as if it were a rack of picture postcards at a roadside attraction overturned by a truculent child and reorganized haphazardly according to the admonishments of some furious dad. Why did Mr. Morse choose to review in this way? Because this is how the nomadic life is organized? Haphazardly, according to the pressures of a grueling economy? Well, we all know how important the top online reviewers are to the future of the industry, and when one of these reviewers, a top-ten online hotel reviewer, strikes a chord, no matter the unorthodox fashion, with a fervent online audience, we can scarcely resist his charms! We hope that tonight, after you get the turn-down service, and after you order the curly fries from the extremely courteous room-service staff, you might read a little here of what hotel life has been like for one man and see in it a reason to book another room, maybe for that spring-break trip you've been planning, that second honeymoon, perhaps, or for Memorial Day. Or maybe just because. After all, everyone deserves a break.

In fact, I expect I'll meet you out there myself one day soon, when we are both on the happy trail of weekend trips to the hinterlands. I'll be the guy with the wife and two teenage children lugging some left-handed golf clubs, looking for the next public course where I might play a round or two. Maybe we could have a drink, or a cup of coffee. We could talk about books! I'll look forward to it.

—*Washington, DC, April 2015*

The Collected Writings of
Reginald Edward Morse

Dupont Embassy Row, Massachusetts Avenue, Washington, DC, October 31–November 2, 2010

There is a style of hotel that we in the reviewing business refer to as *assisted living*, because of its interior stylings, its floral wallpaper, its imperial draperies. An assisted-living-style hotel always has cotton balls in a little ceramic dish in the bathroom, and a scale, because the elderly lobbyists who stay in a hotel like this, lobbyists for the concrete industry or for pork-products trade groups, are constantly worrying about the extra fifteen. The Dupont is one of these senior-services habitations. The bathroom is heavily outfitted with doilies, the counter faux-marbleized in brown, the wall equipped with a magnifying makeup mirror, an essential accoutrement due to the macular degeneration of the guests, and there's a photo, just above the shitter, of the White House. I did not attempt it, but I am certain that you could, while crouching on the shitter and looking into the mirror on the wall opposite, see yourself with the White House hovering just above your head like a sort of pith helmet.

13

We did not belong at the Dupont Embassy Row. K. and myself were far from the senior-citizen demographic. It was the Toast-masters who suggested we stay here so that I could participate in their public-speaking contest, which I had, delivering a speech on the subject of first impressions. The interior of our bedroom there at the Dupont was fine, if small, but it somehow reminded me of my alcoholic grandmother back in Westport and how on occasion, as a small child, I would sit with her on her enormous king bed while she swigged her distilled spirits and did crosswords. It is not possible, at this remove, to reconstruct the stink of decline that was probably indelible in these moments—juniper and toxic waves of grandmotherly perfume—and yet I have a lingering horror of any kind of interior decorating, assisted-living interior decorating, that suggests to me these memories. Too much mustard and brown, and drapery everywhere.

Did I say that the Dupont has cookies on a table in the lobby? I adamantly oppose the attempt to buy hotel allegiance with cookies. Where was I staying just a couple of weeks ago? MA? Or was it OH? Or MI? In any case, another dismal locale where they had individu-ally wrapped cookies on a tray, as if the cookie were enough to curry favor. The cookies in that instance were heavily machined. They had been produced in an enormous airplane hangar somewhere and trucked to this and other identical locations, and the cookies were perfectly chewy. No doubt a focus group had indicated the charac-teristic of the ideal chip-based doughy confection was *chewy*. There was probably some kind of anti-compulsive psychiatric medication liberally added to this trucked-in gross of cookies so that people like me, who could not stop eating the cookies once they were of-fered, would not continuously sneak down to the lobby in the soul-slaughtering hours between two and four a.m. to steal six at a time, finishing most of them before getting back to the room.

Now: The cookies at the Dupont were somewhat different from the cookies at the chain in MA or OH or MI. These cookies here looked great because they had M&M candies in them, in particular red M&M candies, and, being on Dupont Circle, these cookies shimmered with distant reverberations of American political power. The cookies were also timely because we were staying at the Dupont during a major merchandising opportunity—namely, Halloween. But whatever attempted purchasing of consumer allegiance had resulted in the existence of these cookies, which sat on the serving tray next to some moldering out-of-season strawberries and grapes that had probably been recycled from their use as a garnish for a room-service plate two weeks earlier, there was, I need to say, a significant gap between the perception of the cookies and the actual cookie experience. In this case, the cookies, unlike those in MA or OH or MI, were, in the area of mouthfeel, unfresh, and when I am stressing, in a lecture on motivational speaking, how certain words can do a lot for you, *fresh* is often a word I rely on. So I am using *fresh* here with a genuine understanding of its merits. The cookies in the lobby of the Dupont, which had M&M candies in them and looked fresh enough to make any granny happy, a granny who would already be bowled over by the presence of astonishing amounts of wood paneling, golden drapery, and elevators near at hand, were, unfortunately, *unfresh,* more like an arid-desert confection. So as K. and I walked out of the Dupont to try to find a steak joint in the Dupont Circle neighborhood, we broke the complimentary cookie obtained in the lobby into small pieces and flung it over the fence of the Indonesian embassy, thinking that the scheming and warlike Indonesians were probably out at the time, and in the event that the Indonesians had not fed their local squirrels.

Have I mentioned that the lounge at the Dupont was the very

favorite District of Columbia lounge of a historically important
and cadaverous First Lady of the United States of America? Yes,
cadaverous, and given to the horoscope, if you catch my drift.
That First Lady was known to visit this selfsame lounge in this
very hotel where K. and I were staying on this occasion. Perhaps
only twenty-five years or so prior, a mere quarter century, she had
swept into the lounge with her entourage while elsewhere her man
was drifting off into a fog bank of amyloid tangles. Though I am
no longer permitted to visit a cocktail lounge, I did walk down
the dimly lit corridor to the lounge at the Dupont in order to
see the place where the cadaverously thin First Lady once held
court. That the Dupont has preserved itself in that bygone time,
in the image of the 1980s, reflecting the glory that was the cadaverously thin First Lady, is an observation not to be controverted.
The elevators were unchanged, the wood paneling was the same,
the gymnasium was the same, with its barely functioning tread-
mill; the menu had been marked up, price-wise, but was otherwise
probably very similar. The rooms had been rehabilitated, but with
the same assisted-living color palette. Everything there was knick-
knacks and designer chocolates, down to the small canvas bag
containing the hair dryer.

Now, it is true that K. and I tried to abscond from the Dupont
in such a way as to minimize our exposure to the costs of staying, this when we found out that the charge for overnight parking
was forty dollars and that the online connectivity would cost us
twelve dollars a day and that a bagel in the restaurant went for
seven dollars, price points that are somewhat beyond our nomad
budget. I do not recommend attempting to abscond, because it
does put you in a disagreeable relationship with the hotel management. As I have said, I had competed in the Toastmasters
national contest, speaking on the subject of "First Impressions:

How to Make a Good One," a lecture I have delivered with pile-driver-like relentlessness in many regional settings. I had scored high. These days, though, the prize often goes to someone who has triumphed over adversity, someone with a missing limb, or creeping paralysis, or something similar. On this occasion, I also heard speak a certain professional fellow with exchangeable or reversible first and last names, and this professional lobbyist had charm in surplus—he could have talked the entrées in the ballroom off the table—and it turned out that he was the head of some trade association that had to do with, of all things, *hotels*. Although it has taken me more than a year to finalize this, my first posting, I am happy to tell you that this was the moment I got the idea to start publishing online my thoughts about hotels and motels. While listening to the fellow with the reversible names talk about the hotel business. I started taking notes then and there.

Let it be said, however, that though I admired his style, his way with a modifier, K. and I could still ill afford even the incidentals at the Dupont, which, at at least sixty-two dollars, were more expensive than some *rooms* we have inhabited (for example, the Motel 6 on Idaho Street in, Elko, Nevada: fifty-five dollars a night). Having given my speech on the usefulness of the firm handshake and the importance of making eye contact, and having been bested in the contest by others, I did not feel that it was right to stay another night in assisted living, and so I tried to seize my car by claiming a medical emergency featuring acute pains in the lower-right section of my GI tract, halfway between the jutting of hip bone and navel. It could have been a puncture, I told the valet; there could have been a puncture, as I had recently undergone my first routine colonoscopy. Was he aware of the risks of routine colonoscopy? A puncture in the wall of my sigmoid colon, if untreated, could result in peritonitis or, worse, sudden death, because of leakage of the contents of the bowel into the bloodstream. K. manufactured some tears in order to facilitate our expedient relocation. The guy in the garage volunteered to call for an ambulance, but we demurred, saying we could not wait, we had our bags and were ready to go, and that was when some of the management-level enforcers of the Dupont Embassy Row appeared and presented us with the accounting. ★★ *(Posted 1/7/2012)*

TownHouse Street, Milano Duomo, Via Santa Radegonda, 14, Milano, Italia, July 11–13, 2011

I have found on occasion that the Italians are suspicious of the benefits of air-conditioning. Or skeptical, or resistant, or oblivious to the benefits of air-conditioning. Although it is also true that we were lamentably ignorant about Fahrenheit to Celsius conversion, nor would our exhaustion have made such calculations easier. Our trip had included six hours spent in the international terminal at Boston's Logan Airport, where Delta Air Lines, the world's largest, wore us down by putting us on the plane, taking us off the plane, changing the gates, and telling us four different departure times, all of which was followed by the fourteen-hour flight itself, inclusive of a layover at JFK. By the time we arrived at our Italian hotel, at 4:32 a.m. (or, as they say in Milano, 0432), at our wits' end, K. was consternated to the point of tears, especially when we came to understand the still, humid fact of our interior. Did I say that we were staying at the hotel under assumed names, Jonas and Katherine Salk? The air-conditioning was not the only problem. The others I will itemize herewith.

As a general rule, design-oriented hotel interiors should

have some practical sense to them. The sink should make feasible the staging of objects on its edge or beside it. If the sink slopes all the way to the edges, it follows that no items may be put there. The phrenological-skull sculpture on the desk unsettles, and, given that there is one in every room (this we know because we demanded a room change), we might well deduce that the hotel had purchased dozens of these phrenological sculptures. At first we were unclear on the fact that the city depicted in the gigantic wallpaper mural of photos was actually the city we were visiting. Why do we want to look at wallpaper photos of Milan when we could just go downstairs and see the city for ourselves? A faceless and portly middle-aged businessman of Milan massaging some portion of his abdomen, a cherubic boy refugee standing in front of a *farmacia*, etc. We grew tired of them. Yellow rubberized furniture is unappealing. I was in graduate school in sociology during the heyday of the English pop group Culture Club, and I did, I'm afraid, enjoy humming along with their first celebrated tune, "Do You Really Want to Hurt Me?" But playing this, and "Boys Don't Cry," and "Should I Stay or Should I Go?" in jazz versions through the dining-room sound system every day is asking for trouble. Katherine Salk believed that the Culture Club song was what precipitated her migraine, but it could also have been the yellow rubberized furniture.

I didn't realize she was ill until after I tried, at a morning business engagement, to interest some local Italian banks in collateralized-debt obligations—the kind of high finance I'd practiced when younger, before I became a motivational speaker—after which meeting we attempted to make a visit to the cathedral in town and were turned away because, as a *carabiniere* told us, Mrs. Salk was "too discovered." She had to get a lightweight cardigan from the yellow rubberized rack on which were placed some un-removable white plastic hangers, and then we headed back to the cathedral. This while they removed our few belongings to room number 2, where the air-conditioning did perform as advertised. There was a very fat man standing in front of the hotel at all hours with his hand outstretched. He superficially resembled the businessman in the wallpaper photo collage. Mrs. Salk says that the door handles gave her "repetitive stress injuries." And also multiple lacerations. The maid took our unwrapped bars of soap. And: There were people lining up for Hot Pockets, or the Italian confectionary equivalent, under our window, owing to a business adjacent. Was "Do You Really Want to Hurt Me?" an allegory for our relationship to Milan? Some people like a bidet, but Mrs. Salk said she does not want to shoot water up herself from a spigot that others have also used. ★★ *(Posted 2/4/2012)*

Groucho Club, 45 Dean Street, London, Greater London W1D 4QB, United Kingdom, January 5–6, 1998

There are times when it is necessary to be apart from K. for extended periods. Travel almost always marks our intervals of re-flection and monastic separateness. In fact, there was an epoch before K., an epoch in which I was married. It was in those days, on a trip to England, that I first began developing my skills as a motivational speaker, at which I later became a highly regarded professional in the field. Prior to this career epiphany, you under-stand, I plied my trade in the trenches of securities exchange. It is true that the buying and selling of securities is related to mo-tivational speaking, because in each case, I rely upon my powers of observation. When I see an undervalued company, I am powerless not to share the potential for shareholder value. This is an opportunity you cannot afford to pass up; if you do, you will be hitting yourself about the face and shoulders later in life; you will be rending your garments.

That cigar-chomping hemorrhoidal bigot who sits astride the riding mower on the two and a quarter acres beside you, he is smart enough to spend his IRA on this stock, so why can't you? Do you want him to have something you do not? Do you know what will happen if he has something over you? He will come for your possessions, and it will be symbolic at first, he will initially borrow your saw or your dripper hose, but then he will want your car and your fluffy Samoyed, and then, of course, he will come for your wife. Do not find yourself cuckolded! Buy this stock now!

Sometimes this obligation, this intensive search for value, can lead me, internationally, to the old Europe. The Groucho Club, which is a sort of residential club in the City of London, neighborhood of Soho, is noted for the exclusivity of its bar and the eminence of its many patrons. It is true that not all of these persons are financial analysts, but when you consider that the Groucho Club hosts, on a nightly basis, stars of stage, screen, and popular music, then you can understand why I would have been obligated to berth myself there. The networking opportunities were significant. During the nights on which I was present, when I made my needs apparent to a certain bar employee, it became clear to me that there was a Pet Shop Boy on the premises, and while I understood only vaguely what a Pet Shop Boy was, I was even then extremely *chuffed*, as they say in London, about the possibility of talking to the Pet Shop Boy about opportunities that I saw with certain undervalued securities. His support could make all the difference. If it was necessary to *snog* with the Pet Shop Boy or members of his retinue in order to demonstrate the seriousness of my mission, then I would snog.

On the night in question, I was talking with a certain lovely young woman, but mainly as a cover in order to get closer to the Pet Shop Boy—she was in no way a substitute for my wife. In due course, I was alone at the bar, and then I attempted to approach a Pet Shop Boy to ask if it would be possible to purchase him a drink, whereupon he turned on me his gimlet eye (Old Gimlet Eye being initially the nickname, by the way, of Smedley Butler, an American Marine who was at the heart of a coup to overthrow FDR). The Pet Shop Boy's gimlet eye fell upon me, and almost at once there were employees of the bar at the Groucho who made it abundantly clear to me that the Pet Shop Boy was off-limits—*Leave the client be, Yank*—which behavior I do not think argues for the five-star rating that others have given the Groucho Club. It happens that in fact I was staying there in the single smallest hotel room I have ever stayed in; so small was my room at the Groucho, and here I kid you not, that I could open the door to the hallway from my Groucho Club twin bed and likewise reach into the minibar. The television did not require the remote, such was my proximity to it, and one could loft oneself out of the shower and into bed in one supple gymnastic move. Had I been given to claustrophobia, I would have suffered in my room at the Groucho Club. I understand it is the way of these social clubs to cordon off the persons of reputation, and I understand that I am a person who has nothing to offer a celebrity but talk.

This, in fact, was the nature of my career epiphany that night. I seemed to have failed to move enough securities from one account to the other account in order to procure a revenue stream composed of commissions therefrom, and I lacked the resources to short the Japanese yen, but I still had the gewgaws of rhetorical English at my command. I could still *talk* to a Pet Shop Boy, or a Jools Holland, who was also at the Groucho Club during my stay. And perhaps in some way I could make a profession from my language.

I was in a room the size of a coffin, and I survived it by watching rugby on the telly, and the next morning I lugged my rather large bag down the staircase and into the lobby, where I awaited one of the black cabs of London. While I was doing so, a young woman with strategically disarranged mouse-brown locks called to me, "Are you a musician?" To which I replied, "No, I am a motivational speaker!" She further said, "Well, you look like a musician." Which I must say moved me, as just the opposite is the case. And so I replied, "You just don't know the right kind of motivational speakers!" And she: "Top answer! Top answer!" ★★★
(Posted 3/3/2012)

Radisson Hotel, 42 Frontage Road, Waterbury, Connecticut, May 5–8, 2010

Which reminds me of the tendency of hotel lobbies to feature a kind of jazz music that I refer to, despite the fact that K. has asked me to stop saying it, as "smoove." Is there another place on earth where smoove is played with as much consistency as in the lobbies of hotels? Once upon a time, when I was still in the finance industry, I briefly had a car and a driver who came to pick me up at the office and take me home most nights. A fleet of such cars ferried back and forth the mid-level executives of our firm so that they wouldn't have to risk public transportation. Often the driver of that Lincoln Continental, Oristeo, would play something smoove. In those days, there were radio stations of the tristate area that played smoove around the clock—because it was possible that there were people, at any hour of the day or night, who were about to have, or were in the midst of having, episodes of adjustment disorder with mixed anxiety and depressed mood (acute) and as a result were in need of smoove, because the smoove would restore equilibrium. Or sometimes there are somatic conditions that require a liberal employment of smoove in the immediate surroundings of a sufferer. I'm thinking, for example, of long QT syndrome—the thunderous, chaotic cardiac pulsations—which can be caused by second-generation antipsychotic medication, even at the antidepressant-dosage level. K. was once diagnosed with long QT, or catecholaminergic polymorphic ventricular tachycardia, and as a result, on occasion K. would listen to smoove, though this was mostly in situations in which she did not expect to be overheard. Despite what I might have said elsewhere, she was occasionally partial to smoove renditions of, say, oldies like "California Dreamin'" or "I Write the Songs." K.'s affection for smoove became an area of difference between us.

At any rate, we arrived for a stretch at the Radisson Hotel, Waterbury, which was sort of a last-chance Radisson. I believe we had come from a hotel in the Midwest, though one whose particulars I did not choose to preserve for posterity. I recall simply that the lobby of the Radisson featured clocks indicating the different time zones. There was a clock for London, and a clock for Tokyo, and a clock for Los Angeles, as though people lodging at the Radisson of Waterbury were imminently embarking for Tokyo. There were no loiterers in the lobby whatsoever. The bar/restaurant was still open, and there was some kind of forgettable baseball game featured there, on the large screen, with no one watching, and you could see this from the uninhabited and threadbare lobby. The young man at the front desk looked like there was no sorrow he had not experienced, and you could imagine that the pariahs of Waterbury—the convicted frauds and disgraced politicians, the collectors of serial-killer memorabilia, the embezzlers of church donations, those found guilty of exposing themselves, the mortuary assistants with suppressed necrophiliac tendencies, the sadistic gym teachers and embittered traffic cops—all settled here when they were in search of the loneliest night imaginable, and nothing made them feel better than exceedingly loud smoove playing in the lobby. If you were experiencing catecholaminergic polymorphic ventricular tachycardia, some flügelhorn soloing just might do the trick, could render you functionally unconscious in that way that hotel life can often do, unaware of any aspect of civilization that involves continuity, stability, devotion. However, it's also possible that smoove could be seen as a music that requires absolute submission to the American economy, to the need to buy and consume, and, as such, it is straight out of the robber-baron playbook, the music that can and must drive you to your knees so that you can do nothing but purchase plastic trinkets of Southeast Asian manufacture.

We were thinking this as we were checking into the Radisson in Waterbury, and paying in cash, which might have raised an eyebrow. The sleepwalker at check-in did ask us for a credit card for incidentals, because that was the policy of the operation, and we needed to submit to his regime, and so we did, with the resolve that we would *not* purchase any incidentals. K. was much restored when a Stevie Wonder tune came on, recast in smoove. *Isn't she lovely?* By the time the elevator doors retracted, our submission was complete. ★★ *(Posted 4/7/2012)*

Ikea Parking Lot, 450 Sargent Drive, New Haven, Connecticut, October 1–2, 2011

It's true, most people who stay overnight in the parking lot of a big-box retailer choose the more notorious Wal*Mart, and there they make their beds because the political attitudes of the Wal*Mart brand are palatable, even preferable, for these libertarian nomads. K. and I chose the Ikea parking lot not because we felt that it was somehow superior to Wal*Mart but just because we wanted to be closer to the New York metropolitan area in case certain business opportunities arose, or because there was a problem at our residence that could not be resolved satisfactorily between ourselves and our landlord and during which on one occasion I raised my voice in a way that was regrettable, or because my finances were in shambles for several months, or because I needed to amass a security deposit, or because of a legal situation that I may or may not write about another time. Not everyone you encounter while staying in an Ikea parking lot feels as though he or she needs to completely elucidate the *reasons* he or she is staying in an Ikea parking lot. It is enough that there is this dispossession you have in common with your fellow travelers.

The following strike me as important features of parking-lot lodging—should this be your fate. First, the store in question should have inferior security. This was definitely the case with the Ikea of New Haven, which was as woebegone as most of urban Connecticut is and situated directly adjacent to the interstate. Moreover, the Ikea of New Haven had both indoor and outdoor parking-lot areas, so you could sit outside for a while if you wanted to get some sun, and inside if you were interested in additional privacy. Next, the store should have adequate and frequently cleaned restrooms. Any disadvantaged car dweller will tell you this, and during the period in which K. was having a problem with a certain medication, and when we were trying to stay extremely mobile, we came to think carefully about the nearness and cleanliness of various bathrooms in various public spaces and malls, and Ikea, I have to say, had an extremely good cleaning staff. The bathrooms are great. Is there a café? Yes, your store should have a café and it shouldn't be one of those get-'em-in-get-'em-out cafés that feature only Starbucks coffee and some pastry. It should permit loitering. K. and I will forgo a meal or two now and again in order to keep ourselves at fighting weight. But we do like to be able to relax. Recent studies have suggested that thinness is associated with longevity.

An Ikea tends to be huge and laid out like a Vegas casino, so it's easy to give the in-store security, even the plainclothes people, the slip. The store provides a lot of opportunity for walking, which is cardiologically sound. I personally like how much the indoor-outdoor parking lot at the Ikea in New Haven is overrun with birds. There are birds roosting in there all the time. Sparrows, especially. You might think that an Ikea parking lot, if you're stuck in there for a few days, would be devoid of meaningful wildlife, but you'd be wrong. In addition to the birds, I saw raccoons in there, trying to scale some of the dumpsters. And there were squirrels and some rats.

I wasn't sleeping much in the car, an old Saab that I'd bought used not long before. This was just before the demise of the Saab brand. Some cars are more comfortable for overnights. If you were one of those child-abductor types, you would get a van and put a mattress in the back. K. alleges that her ex-husband was exactly that. A child-abductor type. (He was a psychologist, and degrees in psychology, I find, often conceal deviant tendencies. He was one of those psychologists who needed to smoke a lot of weed in order to relax, and he had a ponytail that he often plaited into a braid, among his many other Native American affectations, and he had a radio show on the local college station where he liked to interview sage-burners and New Age physicists. This was in Ohio, which attracts eccentrics, because from Ohio you can travel easily in any of the four cardinal directions.) But back to Ikea: Ikea began its march to world domination in Europe, and in a way it is still not of the United States. As you may have noticed, here we were living in a Swedish car in the parking lot of a Swedish mega-retailer. ★★ *(Posted 5/5/2012)*

Gateway Motel, 260 Maple Avenue, Saratoga Springs, New York, July 29–30, 2011

Yes, in the old days, I did have an actual job besides motivational-speaking gigs: brokerage trainee, institutional sales rep, day trader, and boutique advertiser at a firm in the great city of Trenton, New Jersey. I had a quantitative brilliance. Perhaps it follows, therefore, that I have wagered and gambled over the years. My mind was on the odds on this occasion, see, because we had been at the race-track enjoying the crisp air of an unusually cool summer day and, unfortunately, losing a lot of money, amounts that one probably should not lose, and this was extremely challenging for K., who, as we were driving in this quaint upstate berg after having wagered on the ponies, beheld the exterior of the Gateway Motel and said, *I'm not going in this fucking place, I am not sleeping in here, I told you no more cockroaches, I don't want to stay anywhere with cockroaches, nowhere with cockroaches ever again!* (Why is it that this simple little insect, this hardy evolutionary triumph, the *Periplaneta americana*, can cause such upset in the average motel-goer? Are we not by now

habituated to them? They cause no bite, they inflict no harm except
the occasional germ. All that is required for the nonappearance of
Periplaneta americana is the correct sealing away of foods and rub-
bish containers.) I asked K. where it was she wanted to stay if she
didn't want to stay at the Gateway. One of those Victorian hotels
in the downtown area, all done up in velvet and Adirondack pine,
where the high rollers come in to sip from the top shelf? We were
craftier than that; we didn't need to spend every bit of what we had
in one of those Victorian hotels. The Gateway was the gateway to
the *forest*, a couple hundred miles or more of it. Such was my argument.

With this explanatory rhetoric on my side, I did manage to persuade K. to set foot in a room. And yet, almost immediately upon
setting down our bags, we found a deceased example of *Periplaneta americana* in the bedsheets. You would think that such a motel
would have rates in the $39.99 range, not the $175 range. Admittedly the $175 figure at the Gateway probably had something to
do with the racetrack, with the crisp air, the Victorian tradition of
breakfast at the track, the pomp, the strong feelings of rectitude
that come from slapping down a hundred dollars in front of the
man at the window and betting the trifecta. The ponies! Nothing
says commitment like an opened billfold and the loss that usually
succeeds this opening. On such an occasion, one should pay $175
a night for a room at a motel that is mostly empty the rest of the
year. Still, *Periplaneta americana* is *Periplaneta americana*. Our late-
afternoon nap having been disturbed by *Periplaneta americana*, we
went to the office of the Gateway and struck up a conversation with
the proprietress in which we said we were new in town and did she
have any recommendations as regards dining establishments, but
the proprietress, who had a wandering eye, was cool to the likes of
us and mumbled something about having had her sense of smell

destroyed by a popular nasal decongestant so she no longer had much taste for the finer foods.

Many are the cons that are available to the motel guest who wishes to arrive at a more reasonable price for a room, and over the years we have tried variations on the Melon Drop, the Jamaican Switch, the Sex-Toy Scam, etc., each refitted for the specific hotel or motel environment. In this case, we were using a short con that K. and I had attempted elsewhere, the Nouvelle Cuisine, which involves getting a dining recommendation, coming down with horrible food poisoning, and then blaming the recommender for the illness. This is a simplistic con, I will admit, but I believed the wandering eye of the proprietress would make her more sympathetic and impressionable, and thereby increase our chances. When this did not prove to be the case, K. started in: *Listen, do you know how many bugs are in that room? We have caught some of the bugs, and we put them under the drinking glass in the bedroom that you didn't bother to clean, and unless they are strong enough to push the glass off of them, there's at least five cockroaches still under that glass, and we demand that you do something about them, about the cockroaches, because I don't want to sleep with any cockroaches, and especially because you're asking us to spend $175 on this shithole.* Look, it's worth noting that I occasionally kept in my overnight bag a small glassine envelope filled with four or five mummified *Periplaneta americana,* despite Skylark's dislike of the poor little guys. Would you think less of the author of these lines if he occasionally needed to strategically place the mummified bugs in the room as a negotiating tool, a sort of scourge with which to improve relations with a motel owner?

The proprietress started shouting too, saying if we didn't like it we could just get the hell out (and her perceptiveness about our motives must be admired), and she said this with an accent from some faraway nation, though she had mastered the slang of her adopted land. The argot came so easily to her, *Get the hell out*, and she actually reached out with a rolled-up newspaper and tried to swat Skylark cranially, whereupon I flung up my arm and my windbreaker, which I was holding there, to keep the proprietress from striking K., and I startled the woman. She let out a shriek, and this was enough for Skylark and me to head for the door, and anyone in any of the rooms, any of those compulsive gamblers who were holed up there trying to come up with some more clams, could have heard over the traffic on the county road the cries of "These rooms have cockroaches!" while we ran for the car and drove halfway out of the turnaround before we realized we'd forgotten our luggage...★ *(Posted 7/7/2012)*

Rest Inn, 7475 East Admiral Place, Tulsa, Oklahoma, February 14–15, 2012

The Rest Inn of Tulsa on Valentine's Day. It seems as though this is something that needed to happen to me, one of the top-ten reviewers on the Rate Your Lodging site, with over twenty "helpful" stars from miscellaneous readers. (Thank you, readers!) It is my fate that I should, at last, come to this, the Rest Inn of Tulsa, needing to find somewhere to flop near the Tulsa International Airport. K. and I traveled here, on Valentine's Day, only to find it demonstrably proved that Tulsa is a hard-living place (and *here's* a link to some info, in case you need it, that'll take you to some former addicts of the area, who'll tell you that in parts of Tulsa, there are legions of kids cooking who don't really know, geopolitically, what they're doing when they're cooking, and they're going to purchase bulk amounts of nasal decongestant, and then they're going to come back to this, the methamphetamine capital of the world, according to some law-enforcement sources, and a number of them are going to flop at the Rest Inn on Admiral Place, an ironically titled name for the location of the Rest Inn, and these kids, who are cooking for recreational use, and in some cases blowing themselves up, are undergoing profound vascular changes such that their appearances are drastically transformed, you can see all kinds of self-inflicted facial scarring taking place from the attempted excavation of bugs under their skin, and then there is the weight loss, two weeks without even a microwavable burrito, and the pounds are dropping away, until they have that sort of internment-camp mien, and then there are also the neurological changes that come from the dopamine-release free lunch of the active ingredients, and here I leave unmentioned the dental horrors of this, the greater Tulsa area; there was some lady of Tulsa who tried to manufacture some of the drug inside a big-box store because she couldn't afford to take the raw materials through checkout and into the parking lot, so she was trying to cook it inside the big-box store and was there for six hours, inexpertly manufacturing it, before someone tipped off the police and this lady got hauled off to the county lockup; meanwhile, just about anywhere within a fifteen-mile radius there is cooking, there is lithium aluminum hydride and sometimes hydrochloric acid and lots of other chemicals that you don't want around because they're explosive, and so right there in the Tulsa area, some kids with cognitive impairment and Parkinsonian neurological symptoms, not to mention murderous excesses of self-esteem, are performing advanced chemical operations not dissimilar to medieval alchemical transmutation, although in this case they're not trying to achieve enlightenment, the articulation of self, or even trying to convert base metals into gold, they're just trying to flood the brain with twelve hundred units of dopamine, and in doing so, in cooking, they are pouring hydrochloric acid and sul-

furic acid and lots of other stuff out into the environment around
their trailer, endangering the neighbors, poisoning the ground-
water supply, depressing real estate values, and causing, in the
aftermath of their cooking adventures, EPA intervention in the de-
graded land around their trailer).

Before I tell you about the sketchy characters, and the cameras
everywhere, and the bulletproof Plexi in the lobby of the Rest Inn,
and the way that these impacted our stay, I need to tell you about
a remarkable thing K. said to me on that Valentine's night, while
we were hoping that we were not going to be drug-war casualties
and warming ourselves in the Midwestern chill against each other
between extremely-low-thread-count sheets. (K., in fact, tried to
get through the doorway [where she left her flats] and to the bed
without her bare feet ever touching the floor.) K. said to me, in
the course of our exchanging Valentine's-related pleasantries, that
she had *never experienced trauma*. She put it in a more colloquial
way, I think, saying something like "I've never really experienced
trauma," and this was not, as you might suppose, a slightly fearful
remark about the gun-toting toothless meth gangs of North Tulsa
popping into the Rest Inn to suck on their lightbulb pipes; no, on
the contrary, this was a statement of sanguinary goodwill, a sense
of the rightness of things, of improvement in the world in the
causative locus of K. I did not think the statement "I've never really
experienced trauma" was an accurate statement at all. And if it was
true, it would not be for long. There was every reason to suspect
that our car would be vandalized, as indeed both cars next to ours
appeared to have been, either before or during their stay, and we
had been asked, at check-in, if K. was a runaway or a prostitute and
if we planned on using drugs while we were staying. Under such
circumstances, a certain amount of Halcion or Ambien would have
been warranted, to loft us through the nighttime expanse of those

eight and a half hours. It wasn't traumatic at the Rest Inn, but it was close.

I demanded to know, while I reached for the blackout curtain and pulled it imperceptibly aside in order to watch some guys down in the parking lot loitering in a particularly malevolent way, how K. knew that she'd never experienced trauma, and if she was sure that she was using an adequate definition of the word *trauma*, like, for example, a "developmental emotional wound leading to psychological injury"; she observed that she had taken the Minnesota Multiphasic Personality Inventory, because it was required for a certain research job she had had when she thought she was going to be a CSW—indeed, when she was training to become one— and the test had indicated that in all significant ways, she was a rather normal person, and her memories of her childhood, of when there had been trouble, were of her father sitting down after an argument and inviting the family to hold hands and saying, *Look, there are always times that are hard, but it's our job, during hard times, to look a little deeper, and to try to find ways to love.*

I countered: Aren't there times when an earnest point of view could cause trauma? And isn't it almost guaranteed that fathers who say this kind of thing are either (a) failures in business, (b) evangelical, (c) talk-show hosts, or (d) cult leaders? K., in the calmest way imaginable, the way that endeared her to me, said that in fact it was that particular worldview, which was the post-traumatic worldview itself, that caused the harm, and actually her father was a generous and masculine presence (dead now, so I will never know) whose construction business gave him complete satisfaction and put food on the table, and even his death from metastatic mesothelioma at a rather young age was so long in coming, after the date of first diagnosis, that she had ample time to make her peace with him, and this included playing checkers with him in the hospital and recording and transcribing a lengthy interview with him about fishing, which she then made into a self-published chapbook. I had never been able to verify the existence of this chapbook, and this had made it impossible to execute my plan, wherein I would go online and write several four- and five-star reviews of the chapbook under various assumed names. (By the way, I did find a five-star review of the Rest Inn: "Clean, convenient, and right near the airport! Staff friendly, patient, and kind! Microwave and fridge in room very helpful. There's a Safeway just up the block, so you can make dinner for yourself. Kids loved the pool. You could find a less expensive hotel during your stay in Tulsa, but you couldn't find one with more love.")

Still, I probed K., there must have been something traumatic that had happened to her. First boyfriend sexually aggressive? Nope, he went on to be a sound engineer for Hollywood movies, and he had been very concerned about the number and duration of her orgasms. Was there a pretty girl in high school who tormented her and wrote *slut* on her locker? Nope, the pretty girl had bulimia, and K. felt sorry for her. Hadn't she been in a horrible car accident, or didn't she know some guy in high school who was a daredevil and who, in turn, had gotten into a horrible car accident involving his parents' BMW and a telephone pole and in which several of her close friends from high school were killed? In fact, K. said, in the greater Tampa area, where she had grown up, there was a telephone pole where an acquaintance had died in a car accident, and this had been her first experience with the finality of death, but her parents had encouraged her to talk about what she was feeling, and because her mother was a Reiki practitioner, she (K.) had realized that she was holding a lot of dread of the afterlife in her hips. Her mother had worked on her and had encouraged her to do a lot of hip openers, and then she (K.) had let go, in a welter of tears, of the dread of the afterlife, and while she knew me well enough and cared about me enough to comprehend that I was not going to believe that she had carried a dread of the afterlife in her hips, or that her mother was able to release this dread, it was in fact the case, and because it was the case, she felt comfortable saying that she had never experienced trauma, and because she had never experienced trauma, she was able to be here, in the Rest Inn, at least today, without losing her shit, though she had in the past lost her shit, like that time we were in a foreign country with a malfunctioning air conditioner, or that time we were somewhere with live cockroaches, as opposed to the dead cockroaches that we sometimes brought with us for the Denial of Service con.

This was a very loving way of responding to my inquiry, which, after all, was taking place on Valentine's Day, and it caused me to reach into the drawer where the Gideon Bible was and fetch the chocolates that I had managed to procure in Hot Springs, Arizona. It was a bad night, and I often felt we were in some apocalyptic topography wherein the Islamist rebels were hiding out from the government forces and expecting nerve agents, but I had K. and I had the chocolates, and these were more important than any insurrection.★ *(Posted 8/4/2012)*

Sand Trap Inn, 539 South Hemlock Street, Cannon Beach, Oregon, June 5–12, 2002

The sign advertised artisan-crafted guest suites, and, during my somewhat desperate (and ultimately unsuccessful) trip to interview for an HR position at the Tillamook cheese factory, I was curious to know how the artisan had crafted these particular suites. Did an artisan consist of some slightly inbred white supremacist from the eastern part of the state working on the finish of the handcrafted teak bar in the suite over the course of seventy-two hours, never once needing sleep because of the stimulants employed when energy flagged? Or was there an aging dropout from the dot-com world, someone who had retreated to this charming beach town to work on some artisan-crafted guest suites while transitioning from the dot-com sector, sobbing in the room over the cherry he was using for the desk, whereby he lightly stained the surface of the wood with human tears? There was a subheading on the sign out front that boasted an "in-room Jacuzzi." I wondered, naturally, if the absence of a plural in the matter of Jacuzzis indicated a single Jacuzzi in a single room, the rest of us being, as the saying goes, shit out of luck. Or were there in fact multiple Jacuzzis in which multiple groups of intoxicated golfers and their paid associates could make double entendres until the clock ran down on the Jacuzzi timer. In certain hotels, or motels, or bed-and-breakfasts, etc., it is important to get the proprietor to give you a tour before you settle on a specific room. Often the employees will resist this tour, and you will have to scale the rhetorical heights in order to procure it. Because I am a motivational speaker, I have surpassing persuasive skills. You need to start slowly, in a muted and nonseductive way, using honeyed and time-tested approaches.

As a matter of fact, "artisan-crafted guest suites" were not the thing that moved me to take this room at the Sand Trap. Rather, it was that I saw certain gentlemen on the Sand Trap deck from the street, and I was listening to their conversation, and it was the conversation of these gentlemen that made me want to stay at the Sand Trap. They were not talking about golf, let me say here at the outset. They were talking as certain gentlemen talk when they are really interested in getting to know one another, when they are bent on opening up, and by this I mean, of course, that they were talking about their shifts. My sense is that men of a certain kind, when getting to know one another, will always talk at length about their shifts. You know: *That was that night in July when I pulled a double, a long night, and I wasn't counting on having to go roust some kids who were trying to camp out in the abandoned plant, about as tired as I've ever been, practically seeing double, and those kids had all been drinking, and they really weren't counting on anybody coming along and breaking up the party.* To which an interlocutor can only say, *I had to do a couple doubles in a row one time, I was doing security at the store, overnights, and I had to do a couple of nights in a row, because it was the lady's birthday, it surely was, and I had to come up with some cash pronto to buy her something for her birthday, and I kind of got myself fixed on some jewelry, and so I had to stay up those two nights, and that is what it took.* No particular pathos is ascribed to this overwork, it's just a discussion of the physical aspects of it.

Maybe, just maybe, on certain occasions, a fellow will ask another fellow exactly how much OT he has accumulated in a certain month, but this is usually later in the evening, when all of the possible sports-related conversations have already been depleted, after these men have already traveled to such layers of arcana as when a certain ballplayer will become a free agent, and therefore sports can no longer serve as a topic, then there will come a point when even the shift-related discussion will run out of steam, unless, perhaps, the conversation can extend to a comparison of swing shifts and graveyard shifts. For example, I heard one of these men on the deck, from where I was standing alone on Hemlock Street, totally alone, talking about how he actually preferred the graveyard shift, because he had nothing to get up for anymore, there was nothing in his life worth getting up for, *She moved out, you know, she moved on, said she didn't understand me, that's what she said, couldn't go on if there wasn't going to be even one minute when I expressed any type of kindness to her, and so she was gone, and the kids all cleared out already.* And another guy said, *One time I took the swing shift just to get away from her for a few weeks, I just filled in for this guy who had a back injury, and I came home when no one was awake, and then I'd just take some sleeping pills and drink a few beers.* Everyone had a good laugh.

We were all alike when you got right down to it, myself included, because, though married, I was traveling alone in those days, having very recently extricated myself, at least for the time being, from a star-crossed and athletic dalliance, and so this was exactly the hotel for me, the hotel with the old-fashioned wall-mounted pay phone in the lobby, the hotel with the pool that had been drained of water, the hotel without the minibar, the hotel with the constituency of men who had fallen down on the job or who had had the reversal that they weren't exactly talking about, the men who got up in the morning to shave and greeted their reflections with a few choice epithets, the men who had dreamed big when young and failed more spectacularly to develop these dreams, and when I got to the room, I realized that the artisan was exactly my kind of artisan. There were arachnids in every corner, and you could see all those people walking past on the way to the ice cream parlor or on the way to get saltwater taffy, and there would be no surprises, and the Jacuzzi was just a big bathtub with a few extra jets of water, loud enough that it could cover over just about any cries of despair. ★★★★ *(Posted 9/8/2012)*

The Plaza Hotel, 768 Fifth Avenue, New York, New York, December 27, 1970–January 2, 1971

The proprietors of this web-publishing venture where I have now been posting for several months have expressed a preference that

I refrain from libeling existing establishments and indicated that if my remarks cannot be confined to the merits of the particular hotel in question, they will have to ask me if I would consider posting elsewhere. But I know that you, the audience, are enjoying these essays on the nomadic compulsion, and I know this because while a lot of other people on this site simply vent their particular helping of bile and then move on to post on another site devoted to shoes, or intelligent design, or whatever, unlike those others, I actually have comments beneath my posts (*u r the road warrior reg!*). I read the comments that follow my own, and so I know that there are those of you on whom I have had an impact, and I know that the proprietors not only do not want me to take my opinions elsewhere, but want me to post more, and it is therefore reasonable to assume that theirs are cosmetic suggestions. Am I willing to play ball? Am I a utility infielder, a multipurpose kind of guy willing to tell you about one of the first hotels I remember staying in as a child, if that constitutes a respite from the truth as I practice it here? I am. I am willing to tell you such things, especially when some of you have been so kind as to ask about my early life. (See some of the comments from Dalmatian131, GingerSnap, WakeAndBake, et al.) Perhaps some of this early life material will serve as backdrop to the more contemporary posts above.

My parents were parted early in my childhood. My father was an organization man, and he was often away, and he simply stopped returning to our address after a certain time. No explanation was offered. Or maybe there was an explanation but it was so vague as to be uninterpretable by the likes of me. What a dreadful experience for a young boy who just wanted the company of his dad, who just wanted to whack at baseballs in the backyard with the old man, who just wanted to be taught to use a circular saw, who just wanted to learn the rudiments of five-card stud or blackjack, who just wanted to understand the precise location of the clitoris or how to pronounce *clitoris*, or who wanted to learn how to order meat from a waiter, or who wanted to say the word *meat* with great gusto, or who wanted to learn the proper way to mix and shake a martini, or who wanted to learn to say *good little piece of tail*, or who wanted to contemplate the necessity of moving on, or who wanted to neglect to shave, or who wanted to learn the specifics of firearms, wanted to be able to eject a used shell, to drive with one hand and dangle the other out the window, to belch without shame, who wanted to drink in the morning, who wanted not to bother flushing the toilet, who wanted to learn to walk naked from the bathroom without worrying about who saw him, and who wanted to cut down his colleagues, his personal friends, in midsentence when he had to. Who would not want his dad when his dad was gone?

After a year when my mother often retired to her chamber with aggravated attacks of nerves, she took up with a fellow I'll call Sloane. I come from people whose first and last names are often reversible, and Sloane's first and last names could have been reversed with no loss of plausibility, like Wendell Willkie or Forrest Tucker. Anyhow, Sloane was a guy my mother was fond of, and Sloane had certain avuncular qualities that made him unlike my father, as I remembered him. For example, Sloane did not implore you to shut the hell up, you little fucker, any time you made any noise, like when you trod from closet to bedside in your good shoes. Maybe Sloane tried a little too hard. He did, in fact, attempt to help me learn how to throw a couple of pitches overhand, saying that if I just let my fingers fall off the ball this way, I'd get a little bit of a curve; that is, if I threw with enough velocity. When you're starved for this kind of contact, a little goes a long way.

In any event, we were going to take a ski trip and all I knew of ski trips was that another fellow in my elementary school had come back from a skiing vacation with a compound fracture and a big cast, and everyone got to sign that cast, and they all used those felt-tip pens that were kind of new in those days, and that made this fellow Nicholas a popular lad, because everyone could sign his cast. I was afraid to break my leg, but I surely wanted the attention.

Before we went skiing, though, we went to the Plaza Hotel, which for those of you who do not know is a hotel on Fifth Avenue in Manhattan that is occupied mostly by caliphs from various emirates. Sloane was an entrepreneur, or that is what he liked to say, though I have never met a man who said he was an entrepreneur who wasn't some kind of fraud, but he had a daughter I liked just fine, and we all headed to the hotel. This was my first time in that city I have never quite solved, though I have worked hard at it. Now, I had certainly heard about Eloise, and there was my sister and girlfriends of my sister's who had read all those Eloise books, and I knew the hotel was supposed to be glamorous, and there was the Oak Room, and I ran around the Oak Room, and no one stopped me from running around the Oak Room, where, I believe, I had my first ever Shirley Temple, and if anything gave me the taste for the bliss that is the afternoon cocktail, it was the Shirley Temple and the maraschino cherry. I couldn't even say *maraschino*, but I knew I needed to have it. And then there was the Palm Room, and maybe it was the Palm Room that my sister and I did the running around in, and no one could stop us, because we knew that this would never be ours. It costs, I don't know how much, seven hundred dollars a night for a room? And people can buy condos in there, and back when I was there, probably the only person who lived in it was Elizabeth Taylor or someone like that.

I remember that we stayed over New Year's Eve, and there was some talk from Sloane about going to watch the ball drop in Times Square—Honey, why don't we take all the kids over there?—but my mother had no intention of going along with this, and so we watched it all on television, though we were only fifteen blocks away, and afterward my sister and I went running out into the corridor (Sloane's daughter, the daddy's girl, was long since asleep), because my mother and Sloane were taking no interest in our pastimes, they were in their room, romancing perhaps, and out into the hall of the Plaza we went, and we were free, running up and down the halls, and what other five-star hotel would let the kids of young couples from the suburbs go running wild, looking for Eloise and her staff pals? But we did it until, going around some corner, we were stopped short, and I looked up into the face of some older lady, makeup-less, unjeweled, wearing some kind of nightshirt, her face a lattice of wrinkles, such as might indicate untold wisdom, her face a ballad of experiences, and she held me by the shoulder, now looking right into my eyes, while my gaze took in her diaphanous nightshirt and her unknotted robe, her slack skin, and she said, *Hush now, some of us are trying to sleep through all of this*, and she gestured around. ★★★★ *(Posted 10/13/2012)*

Viking Motel, 1236 North Detroit Avenue, Eugene, Oregon, August 15–19, 2011

My cousin Dennis asked me if I would consider officiating at his nuptial event, and I agreed and therefore needed to find a way to get myself ordained fast. Now, it occurred to me that officiating at weddings was a sideline, a moonlighting gig not at all dissimilar to my primary business line of motivational speaking. What kind of wedding-related oratory, after all, is not motivational at its core? Just about everything that comes out of your mouth in the nuptial theater inspires, transports. It seemed just and right that I should apply to the Infinite Love Church, which is one of those seminaries that ask of you only the eighteen dollars that will thereafter enable you to carry out the sacred rites associated with marriage. The Infinite Love Church requests that you read a few rather sugary pamphlets about their ecumenical views, and then they send you an e-mail confirming that you are in law ordained, after which you are advised to contact the county clerk wherever you are intending to serve to ascertain that an online ordination is considered valid in that state. In this case, the affianced parties were Dennis and his bride-to-be, Olga, of Ukrainian origin. Olga had been in this country since she was seven and had no trace of an accent. She favored brightly colored athletic gear, a little on the baggy side, as though she were trying to hide a third breast. She had read a lot of Dostoyevsky. I learned all of this at a meeting I had with Dennis and Olga, which seemed like something that I ought to do before conducting the nuptial ceremony. If you're officiating, and you're trying to seem as though you are an intercessor, that the Word of God speaks through you, then you had best meet with the parties concerned.

Olga and Dennis came by the motel where I was staying while in town, the Viking Motel. (K. was still mad about the gambling losses in Saratoga Springs. And in this, she was blameless.) About the women loitering in the parking lot, let me just say: That is just youth culture! It's a college town! (Go, Ducks!) And let me say too that Dennis did not deserve the long interval he served in the federal penitentiary for transporting copies of stolen material across state lines, and if anyone was capable of being rehabilitated in the penitentiary, it was Dennis, who met Olga while he was there. It was some kind of epistolary romance, permitted and facilitated by Dennis's job in the prison library. Dennis was a trembly, nervous person, with an island of hair on the front of his forehead, a saddle horn, if you will, with not much else anywhere around it. He was thin and hunched and resembled one of those dogs that you see in public squares in Eastern European countries. Dennis had not found a way to be comfortable in the world. He seemed as though he were habitually preparing himself for something awful, and this was justified because many awful things had happened to him. He said it was because he wore that necklace with the human tooth on it that his father had given him.

At the Viking Motel there was a sign on the front of the vinyl-sided cottage that served as Reception, and that sign said *Back Later, See James in Housekeeping*. I never did see the sign removed. When James in Housekeeping finally did turn up, after Olga and Dennis stood out in the parking lot watching women in detachable skirts marching past, he sheepishly admitted that he had blood he needed to wipe up, and the proprietor never appeared at all, which was why Dennis had trouble finding me, neither he nor Olga having sufficient funds for a cell phone, or so they said. After I had drunk several bottles of beer, or more, awaiting their appearance (this behavior is sometimes called a *relapse*, and K. did not approve), staring at myself in a mirror on the wall by the bathroom that was so large I began to believe that I could walk into it, there was a knock on the door. Oh, mirror on the wall, who has the beginnings of an irremediable panniculus associated with middle age that no amount of dieting can affect? Who has more body hair than a bonobo? I was wearing only boxer shorts, in purple, when the knock came. The hip waders on the cabinet housing the television were for a planned fishing trip in the Cascades area, and I was unwilling to dislodge them to get corduroys out of my drawer. I therefore donned the hip waders. I could see, when I opened the door, that Olga was surprised by the outfit, and I begged her to understand that I was an unsurpassed angler and had a suit at the green dry cleaner up the block, as well as a tie with a naked woman on the reverse side.

Dennis knew me well enough not to be surprised, however, and soon the two of them were sitting on the bed, somewhat uncomfortably. I poured them pop with some ice from the dispensary out by vending and then sat in the lone chair by the window, still wearing the hip waders, which were not suspended properly on my shoulders. I asked them, first of all, if their resolve with regards to marriage was earnest and true and characterized by profundities of desire and mutual support. I told them that marriage, as I had understood it during my own union (come to an end a couple of years before), was a sacred trust, and that many people married because they thought they were supposed to marry or because society expected it of them or because one of them was with child or simply because they were bored and did not know what else to do with their lives. But, I observed, it was possible to do better than this. It was possible to be changed by the revealing light of marriage. In proportion to one's development in marriage, in proportion to the amassing of age-related epiphanic moments, in the habit of love that is marriage, it was possible, I said, for the beloved to become more ravishing, more perfect, as when ascending into the concentric rings of paradise, and that in marriage we come to find the flaws of the beloved less irksome and instead more delightful and endearing—like that weird spitting noise that the beloved sometimes makes when hawking up reserves of toothpaste, for instance, or that tendency the beloved has to nervously scratch her ankle over and over again, or how about her wearing two pairs of socks all the time?

However, as I was saying these things, I happened to look down and notice that because of the odd layering of my own garments—that is to say, the boxer shorts and the hip waders, whose strap had fallen from one shoulder completely, resulting in a sort of bagging of the waders on one side of me and a concomitant riding up of boxer shorts on the other—one portion of the intimate area of my own person was bulging out the side of my shorts, the sack portion of my private self, and while some men have modestly sized testicular containers, I was not one of these men. It was not unknown to me previously, the occasion of that fleshy pouch becoming somehow visible, it was an ongoing problem, and as indeed this was the case now, I quickly looked up, hoping that Olga and Dennis had not glimpsed the bit of me extruded from the shorts via the falling-down and bunching hip waders. Believe me when I say it was one of those wardrobe malfunctions that only chance can bring about. If I could continuously maintain eye contact during the discussion, perhaps I could imperceptibly move the shorts a bit, or the waders, through some kind of isometric hip exercise, so that a bit of fabric would flap over the testicle and its colony of white hairs. I was driven to ever greater heights of rhetorical fancy in order to assure myself that Olga, in particular, continued to make eye contact with me and did not look down. I smiled like a mad person. Any false move or attempt to excuse myself could easily draw her eyes that way. I began looking around the room myself, in the hope that my darting eyes, alighting here on the extra-large sex mirror, there on the stain on the stuccoed ceiling, would likewise seduce her gaze.

I asked Olga if the marital relations were satisfactory, if she could assure me that these relations were characterized by gentleness and intimacy and proper frequency, and there was a surging in-breath from Olga, which at first I worried was because she had finally witnessed my little semi-bald protuberance with its four white hairs fumbling for recognition, but in fact I think the in-breath was owing to the question being a probing and challenging one, and she thought for a while, and then said she believed that the intimate relations were intimate, and she said, as I recall it, *Dennis is a very sensitive man who loves the bodies of women, and I am lucky to have a man like Dennis.* Then I asked Dennis if the relations were sufficient from his point of view, and he said, *In the time I was inside the penitentiary, I came to believe that I might never get to touch the body of a woman again, and so our love is a holy kind of thing,* and here the two of them smiled at each other, bashful smiles of the confederates of love.

Next I asked them about money; I said that it was the lot of some people in the world never to figure out the money problem, and there was no shame in this, because love endured beyond money, and did each of them understand this, and was each of them willing to do the working part, the moneymaking part, if the other was unable physically or was for some other reason unemployed, whether because of felony conviction or ADHD? Olga opined that she had known poverty in Ukraine when it was under the control of the Soviet regime, and her father had for many years had a job as a machinist in which he did nothing at all, he simply showed up at work in a certain dilapidated factory and then came home and spent what little he had on Latvian vodka, and she certainly hoped that the Land of Opportunity would have more monetary reward than that, but as long as Dennis loved her and took her to the movies twice per quarter, then it would be okay. After which Dennis said that he had seen the light about trying to make money by transporting stolen goods across state lines, and now he simply wanted to be, as he said, legit, and if that meant the loading dock, then the loading dock it was. And again they looked at each other and smiled.

In the middle of this smile it occurred to me that I could sim-

ply swipe the ice container off the tiny lacquered side table by
my chair and dash it to the floor; the ensuing mess would di-
rect attention away from the testicle stretching itself languidly *en
plein air,* and I could then rush into the bathroom and perhaps
straighten myself up a bit or at least throw a thin white mildew-
inflected towel over my midsection. This I did, and I'm sure the
swiping motion, in which all the ice went flying toward the door,
did not look terribly realistic, and you can only imagine how distressed Dennis and Olga must have been to think that the man
officiating at their service was a hip-waders-at-night kind of guy,
but there was not time to dwell on this, because the ice was everywhere, and I got down on all fours and began trying to clean it
up, and soon Olga was beside me, and I could smell her perfume,
which she had probably put on just for this evening; in our shame,
we were close together, she and I, we were investigators of shame,
trying to make the most of the moment, and maybe she never saw
the testicle at all, nor the slight varicose vein at the bottom of
the testicle that I had sometimes had occasion to look at; maybe
she hadn't seen it at all, and I do not know why this motel was
called the Viking Motel, and it leads one to wonder many things
about Vikings. They did not last long on this continent, because
of starvation and disease. They quickly headed back to Iceland
and Denmark, in their spiritual devastation, where they could
feud with one another and hack one another with axes named
Head-Splitter and Tree-Foe. What the Vikings had to do with
the Pacific Northwest, I cannot say, as it is my impression that no
Viking ever lived in the Pacific Northwest.

Once Olga and I had cleaned up the ice and I had properly
hiked up the hip waders, Dennis asked if everything was all right,
and if they should be going. I said that I wanted to say something,
and what I said was: *Look here, we are in the Viking Motel for this purpose,*

the purpose of the moment in which you begin your lives together, and I just want to tell you how much it means to me that you have asked me to do this, and I know my father, wherever he is now, and your father were not terribly close, and we didn't have that many opportunities when we were young to spend time together, especially because you lived down south, and I know that you are in a time of need right now, and so I am honored to be the fellow who helps you in your time of need. I have a lot of ideas about how to make this a special day, and I'd like to tell you about a few of my ideas, and I hope you can see that I make these suggestions out of love for you both and out of reverence for the love that you have for each other, and despite my own situation, I make these suggestions out of appreciation and admiration for the state of holy matrimony. And then I suggested that maybe we should have some kind of group hug, to indicate the seriousness of my purpose, and they consented to a group hug, though I had to gather Dennis in like he was a stray sheep and I the shepherd, but soon I could smell his perspiration and his clothes that had clearly never seen much bleach, and I held this couple close and said, *This is the warmth that all good people are looking for,* and that was when Dennis began to edge away. I continued, telling them that I had been compiling a list of things that had been done to me in my own marriage that I thought were inadvisable, that no one should do to another person in marriage, but by that point Dennis had his foot across the threshold of the Viking, and Olga stood beside him, and though I offered them a couple of stiff ones from a bottle of bus-station rotgut, they declined.

My feeling then was of forlornness, of the desperate inadequacies of this human linguistic apparatus that we employ to forestall, a little longer, aloneness, and of how futile these fumblings so often are. In the next lurch of solitude I began trying to add to the list of things not to say to someone in your marriage: Don't ever use a pen while lying on the bed; don't ever forget to put the cap back on a pen after using the pen; don't ever use a pen if it's new; put items in the refrigerator at ninety-degree angles; do not throw things in the bathroom trash if there are already a lot of things in the trash; don't ever lie on the bed, made or unmade, in your clothes; don't get into the bed without having showered; don't put your bag on the bed, don't put your bag on the chair, don't put your bag on the counter, don't put your bag on the table; don't ever do the laundry; don't bite your nails; don't put the toilet paper facing out; don't put the toilet paper facing in; don't accelerate quickly; don't wear those colors together, don't wear *those* colors together, don't wear a stripe and a plaid, don't wear that shirt, that looks bad on you, that looks bad on you, and that looks bad on you, and that looks bad on you, and that looks bad on you too, are you sure you want to wear that, that looks bad on you; please stay out of the house one night a week, please stay out of the house a couple of nights a week so I can have some privacy; don't put that there; don't put that there; that plastic cup was given to me by my grandmother; don't use my towel; don't use my bathroom; you don't understand your own family; you don't understand your own role in your own family; you don't understand what people think of you; you don't understand other people; you don't understand me, you don't understand yourself; I need money for clothes, I need money for credit cards, I need money for school; don't cut your meat on the plate, that sound is awful, cut your meat on the cutting board before putting it on your plate; don't touch me.

And when I was done with this list, which I wrote out on the bed with a pen that I didn't cap afterward, I slumped onto a proper spot on the floor of my room in the Viking Motel and there I took up a close inspection of the carpet's dust, blood, seminal fluid, Ritz Crackers, and insect parts.★★ *(Posted 11/10/2012)*

Steamboat Inn, 73 Steamboat Wharf, Mystic, Connecticut, May 3–4, 1997

Diversity of key and lock design in contemporary lodging is a subject that we need to address, and have needed to address for some time. That there should be some kind of industry standard for how the rooms lock and in the way that you enter the rooms—this does not seem too much to ask. In the old days, you had the little key with the brightly hued tag attached, *If found, please drop in any mailbox.* The postage was guaranteed. You were unlikely to keep the thing for long, because you could easily put it in a mailbox. What was the volume, at the USPS, of hotel and motel keys shipped back and forth across our great land? You can see how the constant duplication of physical keys would be a genuine business expense, because what if you have a guest waiting at that very moment, but the prior guest has run off with the last remaining key? (My favorite keys are the ones in Europe that are attached to little round baubles of lead so that you will not wish to carry the thing around with you. When you depart the premises, you are expected to give it to the philosophy student who is at the front desk overnight. Her hair is blond and straight, her lips are pursed, her English is workmanlike, she has tiny breasts, and she doesn't want to talk to you, she wants to read Heidegger. So you give her the key so you won't be tempted to carry the thing around and have it with you when you are set upon on some small footbridge and deprived of your credit cards and all your cash. As you walk across the bridge with your girlfriend (soon-to-be wife) on this summer morning some months after you met in the wintry Midwest of America, a cute little kid in rags comes up to you and rubs his head against your hip, probably cutting a hole in your handmade Irish sweater, and then his friend comes along from behind and they speak to each other in their impenetrable dialect that you later recognize to be Carpathian. And you laugh at their apparent adorability, thinking nonetheless about how you are not supposed to carry your billfold in your hip pocket, how many times have you been told this? Is it some kind of evolutionary thing, that the Romany urchins are so cute? The kid in front is laughing at you and you are giving him a playful smack on the top of the head while the second one is cutting open your pocket with a switchblade. The whole thing is not meant to go unnoticed—on the contrary, it is meant to be noticed, because there's an art to it, and they want the art to be appreciated—and that's when the diversion starts: this one is a girl, and they're feeling her up or something on another part of the bridge, and you rush toward her to defend her honor, but while you are going to do that, they are making Carpathian comments about your girlfriend (soon-to-be wife). *Aș dori să dracu 'soția lui. Doriți să dracu 'soția lui? Ea are un fund mare. Ea este de mărimea unui automobil. Nu aș ști de unde să încep.* And then you realize they're counting the bills in your very own billfold, your pitiful supply of foreign currency, and off they run in different directions, with your passport too, and you don't know which to chase, and the girl, the dishonored one, is refixing herself and laughing at you as well, and you reach for her wrist, as if she's going to help you somehow, and in that way you come to dishonor her just as she was dishonored symbolically before. You let go of her, and she is fleet, as they all are, and you and your girlfriend (soon-to-be wife) are standing there on the far side of the bridge now, divested of all worldly goods, having been welcomed into this central part of Europe.)

So I understand the development of key cards, I just wish the key cards worked in the same way in each and every establishment. It would not be inaccurate to state that even in the first days of my marriage, there were times when I was asked to vacate the premises, and on these occasions I would stay at such lodgings as were available to me, and mostly these were economy-minded addresses, but on one overnight, for example, I stayed at the Steamboat Inn, which was nautically themed, and it would not be inaccurate to observe that on the evening in question, I could not, in all likelihood, have passed a Breathalyzer test, and therefore it was important for me to book a room quickly at an inn that was within walking distance from the point at which my vehicle, having met a lane divider, had become inoperable. I made my way to the Steamboat Inn, and apparently I was not so impaired that I could not book a room, and I had a line of credit available to me back then that was somewhat more reliable than it became later on, so that I could pay in advance, and so I was shown the room by the innkeeper, who was called Suzanne, after which I went out to try to get some food and perhaps further libation, and when I came back to the Steamboat Inn, at 11:00 p.m., let's say, I was unable to operate the key to my room. I managed to get in the main door, which had not been locked yet, but I could not get into my room.

Now, there are two kinds of people in the world, and the kind of person I am is the kind who under circumstances like this— locked out of his room, unable to operate the key card in the Steamboat Inn of Mystic, Connecticut, not far from the world-famous Mystic Seaport—would elect *not* to go to the front desk to demand that he be granted admittance into his room, for which he has paid $108 (it would probably be more like $195 now), but would be likely, instead, to make do with what was available to him, and so I stretched myself out before the door of my room, to listen to the sound of the HVAC in the hallway of the Steamboat Inn, to hear the inrushing of coolant, the breath of God, *Te-ai culcat din nou, iar acest lucru este patul tău și ar trebui să stea în ea.* So it was until the person came around about 6:45 with copies of morning's *Providence Journal* and gave me a kick, and I was stirred. All of this because of key design.

And so: When you try that card, and that card has, for example, no arrow upon it but rather some kind of advertisement upon it, and therefore you cannot think of what direction the thing ought to be run through the scanner lock, think of me sleeping on the floor of the Steamboat, and when you can't get the little red light to light up green, think of me, and when you get the thing turned around the wrong way, and you're on the twenty-third floor, and you're going to have to go back to Reception, think of me, and when you demagnetize, think of me. Do not, I have been told, carry a credit card near your key card. Do not carry a cellular telephone near your key card. Do not carry keys near your key card. Do not carry quarters and dimes near a key card. I have even been told that the magnetic field of the human body can demagnetize a key card. Demagnetizing is a fact of life. Which means that on occasion, the subatomics are at work. Atoms are mostly space. ★★★ *(Posted 12/8/2012)*

The Equinox, 3567 Main Street, Manchester, Vermont, October 1–3, 2001

Of the use of the lodgings of North America for illicit liaisons we must now sing. The popular sentiment is that these liaisons occur mainly at motels noteworthy for hourly rates. But this is prejudice, because who does not commence his illicit liaisons in landscapes of affluence, power, and repose? Once upon a time, I was infatuated with a certain professor of the language arts, as they call them now, and this professor was lodged with presumptive tenure at a certain former girls' college in the southern part of a New England state, and in due course, this infatuation became a searing, abasing sequence of illicit liaisons. One of those days, one of those occasions, had to be the first illicit liaison, the first such event, which is in retrospect like the time-lapse photography of flowers opening to the dew, or like the chrysalis in which the caterpillar performs its striptease and emerges as the *Hyalophora cecropia*. So much work, most of it in the area of self-deceit, has gone into the preliminaries necessary for the illicit liaison, and you can see the principals convulsed in want, waiting for the decision to be made, tying themselves into such involutions, such elaborate confections of self-deceit, that it's as if they will never again be able to stand still, and it's a wonder they can even do a small thing, a picayune thing, like post a few simple comments on an online rating service, so overcome are they with the agitations of their illicit liaisons.

And so it came to pass that we found ourselves in front of a massive hotel, a massive, ridiculously colonial thing, of the sort that no man on earth could possibly fund anymore, such that it must be owned by some latter-day plutocrats, because the place is never full, even in the skiing months. It must have three hundred rooms, because it takes ten minutes to walk from end to end on the main floor, and out on the sidewalk there are these beautiful streetlamps that I believe were the first streetlamps ever installed in the United States, and then there are all these outlet stores just down the block, and you can see them coming from miles around, the buyers heading for the Ralph Lauren outlet or the Giorgio Armani outlet.

It was leaf-peeping season, and the language arts instructor and I had been driving aimlessly in the absolute bliss of illicit congress, the transformative overwhelm of the forests of that New England, the New England of my own early years. We found that we could drive to the top of a certain mountain nearby, and so we drove, not worrying particularly about how the brakes of the rental car might burst into flames on the way down. No, we drove to the top of that mountain, which in any other American state would be considered a foothill, and on Mount Equinox, we surveyed the riot of color and decay, the instructor in language arts and myself, and we didn't feel we had possession of all we saw, we felt that we were *swallowed* into all we saw, and at the end of this, it didn't matter who was married to whom, it mattered only that we shuck off our outer layers, that we abandon our fripperies in the nearest hotel.

There are many lodgings in this part of New England, true, but as new lovers do, we *threw caution to the wind*, and we picked the most expensive one we could find, and we determined that we would just walk in like we owned the place, because we believed that we had become one with the natural world, all things were as they were supposed to be, a beautiful colonial-era mansion, the virtuosity of autumn. The language arts instructor told the teenage clerks at the front desk that she was pregnant, and she would like to have a room as soon as possible so that she could lie down, which was a pretty amazing fib, especially under the circumstances, and I loved her for it! And I'm not going to say that the response was such as to make the room immediately ours (the only black mark against an otherwise sterling reputation for service), but in due course a room was found for us, and it was lovely and paneled with the wood of local conifers, and there was springwater on a side table that somehow you could imagine came from an actual spring, but it was almost lost on us, as were our surroundings entirely lost on us, because that is the way of those illicit liaisons, which is the selfish part of the whole thing, the part where nothing matters but what you think you have to do, and so we were like some tornado on the plains as we cast off the exterior layers of identity and civilization.

Now, I should say (and it's rather delicate to say, but for the sake of the review I will say it, because there is nothing that I will not say for the sake of the review, because the truth of the review is everything, as is the accuracy of the review) that the language arts instructor did not tell me something important, she didn't tell me that as regards a certain time of the month, certain blood rites were hers, she was a veritable fountain of blood and had been known to warn people (she later told me) when that day was present, because not only was she doubled over in pain some of the time, but she also bled like the proverbial stuck pig. It was so overwhelming that there was really nothing to do but give in to the experience of the blood, and, intermittently, make it a part of the experience; she had even (she later told me) insisted on more than one occasion that certain partners in crime wear some stripes of the stuff on their faces as an indication of the seriousness of their devotion. I would have considered myself somewhat apprehensive about the fountain of gore, even though it is certainly bad form to be apprehensive, but see my comment about truth and accuracy above. I had not been informed, so we shucked off our outer layers (I believe I was wearing an olive-colored corduroy jacket, a white oxford-cloth button-down shirt, and some denim pants), and she excused herself briefly, she and her mane of dirty-brown asymmetrical hair and her leonine prowl, which only heightened my anticipation there in the Equinox, and then she emerged, some glorious creature, ready for the assignation, and we assumed some highly combative positions on the white sheets of the Equinox. The extremely white sheets. The white sheets of the Hotel Equinox that were probably labored over at great length by a crew of teenagers down in the basement.

Almost instantly, I could feel the fountaining of liquids in the middle of the illicit liaison, but I did not care, because I was careless at that moment, and we did what we had lied to ourselves about doing for months, and what would certainly hurt a lot of other people, and what was bound to occlude all honest and open conduct in our lives for months, if not years, to come, and we finished up, and, well, there was blood everywhere. I suppose we could have put down a towel, as people do on occasion, but then there would have been blood all over the towel. As it was, there was blood all over the midsection of the language arts instructor, and, likewise, there was blood all over me. I certainly looked as though some part of my anatomy had been, if not sundered from me, then at least badly distressed, perhaps bitten in some way, as though by an animal. Blood everywhere! We got up from the bed, realizing that we had covered the aforementioned white sheets, and dashed into the shower hoping not to spill any more of the blood, and there we laughed like young lovers, though we were not young, and cleansed ourselves of the immediate evidence of our crimes. And then the language arts instructor—brazen in a way I could never have been—called down to the front desk and asked for re-placement bedding. She balled up the bloody set and left it right out there in the hall. There was a knock at the door in a very short time. ★★★★ *(Posted 1/12/2013)*

The Mercer Hotel, 147 Mercer Street, New York, New York, May 5–7, 2002

Hair-care products are an important part of any lodging experi-ence. A seasoned traveler, that is to say, a person who is never home, a person who's putting up at an expensive hotel with a language arts instructor while his wife (I regret to say) is in an apartment no more than two miles away, is in a position to profit in the area of travel-size hair-care products. I know that there are readers who believe that a guy with my particular tonsorial stylings—which is to say, with very short hair where there is any hair remaining—does not require conditioner, because what is the purpose of conditioned hair if you don't really have much hair? But I say that these critics, these abnegators of the creature comforts, do not know of the pleasure one receives in checking into a very good hotel and finding that one can fill one's overnight bag with superior hair-care products, including a rosemary-scented conditioner that makes one's scalp tingle. The lavender-scented body wash—or was it verbena?—was also a nice touch, and while I usually disdain body wash, I do not disdain an opportunity to try these products in the privacy of my own home at a later date to see if particular brands meet my needs. If you travel enough, you can get jars and jars of this kind of thing.

Now, the Mercer Hotel, where I was ensconced with the language arts instructor on the dime of her husband the arbitrageur, is the sort of hotel where you are liable to see the occasional movie star, but I do not pay attention to this sort of thing, and I would actually see the presence of movie stars as negatively correlated with a premium lodging experience, because the presence of actors or celebrities brings with it the presence of the kinds of people who want to be seen with or otherwise be in league with celebrities, and these para-celebrities swarm around the hotel and deplete it of hair products and other amenities.

The language arts instructor, it emerged over time, had some kinks in the delivery of romance that were unlike others I had encountered and were, in a word, disturbing. The language arts instructor, whose arbitrageur husband believed she was staying in Brattleboro for a departmental conference, liked to be lightly strangled during the practice of certain advanced kinds of venery. I cannot exactly recollect how she told me that she wanted me to strangle her a little bit. I don't know how the strangling got introduced into the conversation, nor do I remember if there were explicit instructions as to how I might strangle *a little bit.* But we were on the floor of a room in the Mercer, and I was able, in those days, to get up off the floor more easily than I am now, so being on the floor does not sound entirely ludicrous. (And I should say that the rooms in the Mercer are incredibly clean, so the floor was not such a bad place to be, and I don't recall any rug burns.)

I remember trying to accommodate the language arts instructor, and while we could have been talking about the language arts or the department, instead, she seemed to want to be asphyxiated, though I also thought that perhaps she just wanted to feel like there was someone who disliked her enough to strangle her, and while I didn't know if I loved the language arts instructor, I did think that holding someone and watching her shudder with pleasure, as occasionally happened in the pursuit of illicit affairs, did increase your appreciation of the person, especially if you did it frequently enough, and so I found that I could not, in any convincing way, strangle the language arts instructor, or simulate strangulation, even if that was what she wanted in order to take it to the next level, as she called it. I tried to do what she asked, in the Mercer Hotel, while somewhere nearby, mere floors away, Benicio del Toro was taking a meeting with some midlevel producer, perhaps about a biopic concerning the life of Che Guevara, and so there was a kind of a pause in the illicit affair while we took in the information that I could not strangle, asphyxiate, or otherwise constrict the airway of the language arts instructor.

We repaired to the bathroom instead, and while you grow to assume that bathrooms in the city of New York never have generous tubs, this one did, a tub big enough for both of us to get in, and, after a few jokes and the passing back and forth of some hair-care products of the kind mentioned above, the language arts instructor, with her back turned to me while she soaped up and dunked herself, began to shudder and weep, and said, *You have no idea how painful my marriage is, you just have no idea. I just can't bear to go back there, to the house.* To which I said: *What can I do? How can I help?* And she said: *You can't do anything, nobody can.* And then she wept for a while longer, and I held her around the back, held her to me, in a kind of encircling, but not a kind of constricting, and she did have an incredibly beautiful back, just as almost every other part of her was beautiful; there were just enough flaws to make her perfect. But after a while I got bored of the tub, as one often will with shared baths, and therefore I got up and out of the tub on the pretense of getting her more premium bath salts, and I went out to the bed, hoping that she could compose herself so that we could be people who troubled each other as little as possible. I listened to her going through some sequence of ablutions, and then I listened as the water circled down the drain.

It came to pass that she called to me: What should I wear to bed? And this must have been a rhetorical question, because what should one wear under these circumstances but either (a) nothing at all, or (b) something that is suggestive of and/or preliminary to nothing at all, meaning something barely substantial and yet expensive and black, or perhaps red, but instead I said: *Let me see your pajamas. I want to see your pajamas.* To which she said: *No way, no fucking way, why would I let you see me in my pajamas, you won't want me anymore.* And I said, *Don't be ridiculous! I love everything about you! I'm crazy about you! I want to see you in your pajamas because I want to know about you in your pajamas, I want to be someone who knows that about you, and if that's a vulnerable thing, then that's a vulnerable thing, all the better. I want to love you even in your pajamas.* There was some rustling around in the bathroom, which, as you know, is a very agreeable rustling to listen to. *Which color?* she said. *I have pink and I have black.* I said: *Pink.* It could have gone on this way for years. We could have turned up at dozens of places, dozens of hotels; she could have accompanied me during my training in motivational speaking, come to the conventions I went to, she could have come on some of my corporate retreats, we could have become parts of each other's lives so that it was impossible to tease us apart if only she hadn't agreed to wear the pink pajamas there in the Mercer Hotel. Because once I saw her in them, I loved her in the same way I love my sister, which is an impasse of the truly impassable sort. ★★★★ *(Posted 1/13/2013)*

La Quinta Inn, 4122 McFarland Boulevard East, Tuscaloosa, Alabama, January 5–9, 2002

Under circumstances of regret, during the long nights of regret, you should be back at home, but you are not back at home, because you have to go somewhere you don't want to go, somewhere no one should have to go, namely, Tuscaloosa, Alabama. Well, sure, you can go there without incident if you are fervently interested in things gridiron, and you can go stand on the lawn and watch as the twenty-year-olds with the shaved heads pass down the main drag along the campus in their flatbed trucks, waving their bruised fists. Oh, look, there is the tight end; oh, look, there is the safety. Another winning season. If you are interested in things gridiron, your heart will rise up at this address. If not, this will not be your experience. I wish I had never been there. I will never again go to Tuscaloosa, I will not go to La Quinta on McFarland Boulevard, no one can make me unless I can be assured that each day in Tuscaloosa I will be served grits. And I do not mean cheese grits. Were it not for the tasty grits, I'd be happy to permit the southern part of the country its long-delayed secession.

And yet, on one occasion I found myself at La Quinta, which has good access to the interstate highway system, isn't far from campus, and—if you are not selling auto parts or rug samples and do not believe in a personal Redeemer—makes you feel like you are at the edge of the known universe, hastening away from all that is good and civilized. When I wound up at La Quinta, having been hired as an independent contractor by the major-gifts department at the university, charged with putting on motivational workshops for the staff, I looked deep into my heart and found that there was nothing there, that I had become like an expanse of synthetic-fiber wall-to-wall carpeting. My paralysis was complete, and all I could do was watch television and pop pills from the vials given me by the language arts instructor, who had a lot of vials of, for example, Wellbutrin and Zoloft and Klonopin and Ambien.

The list of Ambien side effects includes headache, depression, sleepiness, and profound personality change, and nearly all the literature suggests that you should call your doctor if, while taking Ambien, you have a profound personality change, but the question, in this rearview mirror, is whether the profound personality change I experienced in La Quinta in Tuscaloosa was caused by the Ambien or by La Quinta itself. For example, the interior decorating of La Quinta could in fact cause profound personality change, as this decorating had a nauseating insistence on what I like to call Mexican pastels, perhaps owing to the chain's origins in the state of Texas, and I have to say that earth tones, at least for me, certainly brought about profound personality change, as did the absence of a dining facility, and I'm not going to say that the breakfast nook was sufficient to scratch that itch. So if we were attempting to isolate possible causes of profound personality

change, we could speak of the presence of Ambien in the bloodstream, or we could point to La Quinta itself, or we could remind
the reader about aggrieved heartbreak. But what about Tuscaloosa
itself, with its pro-life billboards and its relentless fraternities and
sororities? Could this not result in profound personality change
in which a person who was normally sunny, upbeat, kind, and entirely positive found himself feeling like throwing himself under
one of those flatbed trucks?

It bears mentioning that part of the period at La Quinta in
which I was supposed to be conducting empowerment workshops
took place during, or just after, what appeared at the time to be
an irremediable separation from the language arts instructor, before subsequent instances of recidivism, and there were occasions
during this stay when, in the breakfast nook, I found myself bury-
ing my face in my hands, stifling sobs, while a fat guy with a
crew cut got his pancakes and drenched them with syrup stored
in individual packets, and his pal Don, the one with the galloping
rosacea, piled high a plate with more breakfast meats than I have
ever seen a man take, and they then proceeded to talk about another fellow in the office who just absolutely would not give up
his habitual parking space to the woman in Accounts Receivable
who had just been classified as an American with Disabilities because of her rheumatoid arthritis. This conversation crossed the
fifteen-minute threshold. I listened because how could I do otherwise, and somehow in the course of the discussion, there was a
joking mention of unwanted back hair—here was a type of lev-
ity that might have indicated that these two men were reasonably
aware of the shortcomings of their lives and habits—and yet I
buried my face further in my hands, thinking about the language
arts instructor who, after having accompanied me to Tuscaloosa,
had returned home early following multiple instances of chas-

tisement of my person (for such is the way of romance, which, until K., had always seemed to me the success that was an interval between failures) and about the poor attendance at my empowerment workshops, all the while taking in the fact that though there was a breakfast nook and this was the Deep South, there were no plain grits at La Quinta, only cheese grits, and as I have already said, it is not possible to consider a serving of cheese grits as falling under the rubric of grits.

What about tradition? The tradition of coarsely ground cornmeal, which goes back as far as the natives of this country? I understand that there is a tendency in an evolving economy to want to tinker with tradition, to tinker with greatness, but the addition of cheese stretched this elemental food beyond its proper range, and it could be considered fit only for the expanding belt lines of an ever more obese local populace.

I was suffering with profound personality change, and if I had to go out onto the highway and stick out my thumb and secure a ride to a Waffle House in order to consume grits in Tuscaloosa, Alabama, I would go to a Waffle House, leaving behind the unwanted back hair and the expanding belt lines and the godforsaken cheese grits to make of myself a person of the road, a person of the highway, a person of indeterminate location. You could get some grits at a Waffle House, and it wouldn't cost you an arm and leg, because it was presumed at Waffle House that you were on your last nickel, that you had squandered opportunities, that all was illusion. A man still has to eat, however, and coarsely ground cornmeal was best. It needed nothing other than what it was, and if an inn with a bunch of nauseating pastels and some faux-Mexican decor could not provide you with true and authentic grits, then you might go elsewhere, as you did, eventually. ★ *(Posted 3/9/2013)*

Union Station, Water Street, New London, Connecticut, May 13–14, 1984

How grateful I am that you guys have named me a top reviewer on this site! You and I are people conjoined by a belief in sincerity and by a basic agreement about what that means. I'm not going to say the hair dryer in the room didn't scorch a hole in the wall if it did. That's just who I am. Say you are staying in a hotel room in Hilton Head, South Carolina, that was used shortly before you took occupancy for the filming of an adult movie, perhaps because of the sybaritic amenities of the hotel and the appearance in the backdrop of southern vegetation, such as Spanish moss. Don't you want to know that this is the kind of hotel that allows such uses, the kind of hotel that might clean up a little bit and spray around some disinfectant but doesn't bother to eradicate the condom that is draped across the desk chair that had been wheeled into a corner so that the makeup girl could linger there before applying more concealer to the buttocks of the principal actress?

Which reminds me: I have often desired to have an infrared camera of some kind that could detail the dried, encrusted seminal fluid that is surely concealed on hotel-room bedspreads, which we all know are not routinely cleaned. Should we not be trying to create a national conversation on the subject of cleaning the unlaundered bedspreads of the world? I think there should be a referendum on the laundering of those bedspreads. Is it not worth saying aloud, if you are a well-respected reviewer on a well-respected hotel-rating website, that the fact that we accept these bedspreads as reasonably clean is hard to fathom? Is this just where we find ourselves, in a world where the bedding in every unregulated public space is heavily encrusted with dried seminal fluid? It's true, the sheets were changed this morning, the old ones taken down to a subterranean cave where a group of Hispanic women stirred the sheets in gigantic vats of bleach and probably threw in frogs and newts and cursed you and your Gringolandia, but your bedspread has been in touch with chlamydia, scabies, human papillomavirus, and crabs, and on that bedspread two college students who borrowed their parents' credit cards and charged the night's lodging (in order to get away from their roommates) made four hours of furious love without bothering to peel back the bedspread, because their urgency made the peeling back unnecessary, and maybe you lie awake some nights in your hotel wondering why you do not have the urgency that the college students had, but that does not mean you want to sit on that bedspread, or put your windbreaker on that bedspread, thereby coming into brief contact with the vermin cataloged above.

My own college career, which was spotty and episodic, mainly took place in the so-called college of life, also known as "The Land of Steady Habits," and on one occasion close upon my graduation (which took place in the seventh year of my undergraduate studies and had involved a lot of moving around between departments: premed, English literature, philosophy, and then business), I traveled a little farther to the east of the Nutmeg State in order to try to make contact with a girl on whom I had some kind of feverish and mostly imaginary crush. The girl in question was staying with her family on Long Island, and I determined to take a ferryboat from the run-down and hard-luck town of New London, Connecticut. There are roadhouses upon roadhouses in New London. And a very few strip clubs, and a lot of people with missing limbs. I was young and poor, and I was bent on love the way a crow is bent on a flattened squirrel, and so I made my way to New London, regardless of the lateness of the hour; no, perhaps because of the lateness of the hour. I climbed down from the

Amtrak train at Union Station and jogged toward the ferry company's ticket office, carrying (clumsily) my overnight bag—whose zipper had long since given out and which was now closed only with safety pins—desperate for reunion with this girl (I'm leaving out her name), only to find that the last ferry of the evening had already left.

Suddenly, I had a lot of time. The temperature was not exactly as balmy as it ought to have been for a night in May, and, as I recall, the moon was gibbous. I walked into one roadhouse and feared for my life and I walked into a second roadhouse and feared for my life and so returned to the train station, only to find it closed and locked. I had no money and no protectorate, and there was nothing to do but find a place there by the station to wait out the night and reevaluate my plans in the morning. This was the time before mobile telephony. I was young, in love, and free, and so I settled down beneath a shrub. No doubt the local authorities assumed that I was like other drifters of that town, all of them protesting their waning relationship to New London's once great whaling operations, or I was perhaps obsessed with the nuclear submarines across the river Thames. In any event, there I slept for several hours, with no worldly possession that anyone could take from me, with nothing but my earnestness for any who should pass by. I don't want to tell you what happened later the next day with the girl. ★ *(Posted 4/13/2013)*

Emerald Campsites, 1373 Route 9, Corinth, New York, June 24–27, 1991

I once worked at a summer camp. It had one of those unpronounceable Indian names, and it was located near the mighty Adirondack

Park. I was the head counselor of the junior section, exceedingly adult by summer-camp standards, and these kids, many of whom must have had families staying in the vicinity for the summer, were affluent. They would come for the day, do hiking and sports and a little nature identification, have some chipped beef on toast around a campfire, and then head home. Our workdays were in the ten-hour category, and when they were over, most of the counselors needed to let off a little steam, which often involved sodden nights of drinking at biergartens in the Lake George area, where you could also see the tallest freestanding Uncle Sam in the Lower Forty-Eight.

It's important to mention two things about my time at the summer camp with the unpronounceable name. First, I was, in that period, associating myself with Irena, the beautiful and high-strung daughter of a neurologist. Her neurologist dad had been a child in hiding in Poland during the Holocaust, stuck in a basement with his sister for eighteen months, nothing to read except Christian scripture while his parents were off being killed by the Nazis. Her father, gentle, brilliant, and full of barely suppressed feeling, was in many ways the opposite of Irena, who was whippet-thin, given to tempers of startling adamance, and jealous far in excess of what could be borne. Had she been a man, Irena would have been the kind of guy who makes his girlfriend wear a tracking device when she goes out for groceries. That's the first thing about my time at the unpronounceable camp: Irena.

And the second thing about my time at the unpronounceable camp was Monique. Five or six years older than I was, Monique taught pottery at the summer camp. She was tall, quiet, easygoing, with hands like a lobsterman's and a sardonic sense of humor. She was always covered in glaze and crumbs of clay. Monique and I had not consummated our intense fondness for each other, and

I mostly stayed clear of her when I could, ducking behind trees and claiming other engagements whenever we chanced to pass, an easy enough excuse to make because I did in fact carry a clipboard and a golf pencil and was always looking for, say, a camper who had sprayed his shorts with aerosol, set them on fire, and was now attempting to don them. One night only, after Monique and I had sat by the canoes trying to recite as many children's books from memory as we could, I seized one of her hands (which is why I am able to describe them in detail), crying out with gratitude, and then, before I knew what I was doing, her hand, as if I could take it away from her, was in my lap, and I was holding it and studying it, and she leaned in to make this possible, and there we sat in silence, doing something fabulously erotic, at least if you are permitted nothing else by reason of a jealous daughter-of-a-Holocaust-survivor girlfriend.

Next day, Irena arrived for her weekend visit. She drove a Volkswagen Rabbit, despite the fact that the Volkswagen corporation was well known during the war for using slave labor, and the car had a hundred and fifty thousand miles on it, no rearview mirror, problems with the transmission (you needed to start it in second gear), and a driver's-side window that would not go up all the way. Irena liked to camp. Despite the fact that I was working at a summer camp and often took the kids up a hill at rest hour to bed down in a lean-to that we had erected for this purpose, I personally hated the outdoors. I cannot count the number of ways I hate camping, though the foremost reason is this: While camping, there is always a root sticking into the lumbar region of my spine during the night hours. A hundred air mattresses have I inflated during my life, and under no circumstance, air mattress or not, have I ever managed to steer clear of the root in the lumbar region. You are always, when camping, waking at some hour and trying to find a slightly different spot that does not feature a root or igneous outcropping.

In any event, Irena, because she was thrifty and liked camping, had already selected a fine lodging for us, namely the Emerald Campsites of Corinth (emphasis on second syllable), New York, which did enable RVs to pump out and did have hot showers available. (I guess in those days it was still not impossible to get a cold shower at the campground.) There was a barn on the property in which there were a few amenities, such as a soda machine, and then there was a doublewide where the owners of the property could be scared up, if needed. Almost all the campers there, when we pulled in, were RVs, and we picked a campsite for our tent that was as far from the RVs as we could get and still be on the site. The woods were carpeted with pine needles, thick with this carpeting, and very quiet, or maybe it was just quiet because I was there without a large group of ten- and eleven-year-olds, each bent on the candy bars that I had hidden away for them after rest hour. It bears mentioning that upon seeing Irena, the waves of guilt that I was feeling for having held Monique's large, gnarled, clay-besmirched hands were intense and powerful. But I would have done it again just the same, and I later did. Having erected the tent, I was meant to perform some simulation of re-union with Irena while thinking about gnarled, clay-besmirched hands, and to tell stories of summer camp, the various brats with their various charms, without talking about Monique. This was scarcely possible.

We had to find something to do other than sitting out there in the quiet of the woods failing to make love, and so we ambled down into a grove of pines to the red barn, and there we spent some quarters on a couple of carbonated soft drinks, and we noticed that in the barn was a Ping-Pong table. It happened that I was rather a good Ping-Pong player and had been playing recently with one of the other counselors who was from China, where it wasn't called Ping-Pong. He held the paddle in that Chinese fashion and was extremely gifted with spin, as though Ping-Pong were particle physics. And so Irena and I played the sport of table tennis, because I was freshly schooled in it. I could not but win.

After a couple of games, a screen door slammed up at the doublewide belonging to the campground's proprietors, and a certain species of uncle lurched out wearing a T-shirt that did not quite cover his prodigious beer gut, which overspilled some baggy jeans that could not be compelled to hang around his abundant waist. He had a Narragansett beer, foaming over the lip. He must have heard the tinny carom of the Ping-Pong ball; he must have been lying in wait for it. Did I say that he was indisputably drunk, completely potted, staggering, slurring, incoherent, but nevertheless totally bent on challenging me on the Ping-Pong table? He must have believed, the uncle, that his drunkenness somehow improved his game, and that was just one of many delusions associated with his alcohol-related disability. Irena turned over her paddle, and the uncle made certain gestures that I interpreted to mean that the game had now commenced. As would likely be the case under these circumstances, the uncle could not play well. While he had a way of winding up to serve that must have been graceful once, in some prior decade before the advance of his alcoholism, by the time he was playing against me, this windup was more residual than helpful. He missed the ball frequently, he couldn't serve, his table coverage was minimal. And his slam, which grew more urgent the more lopsided the score became, soon acquired an edge of irritation, even coiled anger. I was worried that my purposefully throwing some points would be recognizable to the uncle and that he would interpret this as a kind of disrespect. But, fortunately, he was so wasted that I got away with it. I swatted at a few things that sailed the ball off into the recesses of the barn, and the uncle had to go root around in the dirt and straw, happy, nonetheless, that he was on the scoreboard.

Of course, I pummeled him in the first game. I don't believe he got to double digits. Still, he wanted play again, and then when I threw even more points, watching Irena watch the proceedings with a nervous, gaping anxiety, I won again, and then won a third game, and still the uncle would not give up. Rivulets of infected spittle streamed down his chin as he tried to concentrate in ways that divided him from his fog bank, so that he appeared to be watching himself fail, in a state of curiosity and mounting shame. Which caused him in turn to suck on his tall boy all the harder. The light was failing in the barn, and a few kids had happened along to watch as the uncle went down to ignominy, and maybe they were happy about it, because he was a drunken wretch, and he was unpredictable and treated them poorly. At last, after the fourth game, at which I was also victorious despite my efforts to be otherwise, I said something about how we had to get some dinner, and we left.

Irena and I whispered, gasped, and stifled cackles about how laughable the uncle had been until we got back to our tent, made cheese sandwiches by Coleman lantern, and then, in each other's arms, tried to sleep. In the forest, you know, though it is the placidest location of anyplace, it's hard not to think about murder. In the silence there is murder; in the murmuring of night owls there is murder; in the occasionally snapped twig caused by some fawn happening by there is murder, and it's worse when you have just beaten the alcoholic proprietor, not just once but four times, at Ping-Pong, and all you can think about is that he knows which campsite you're squatting on, and if he wants to come by with his chain saw, he can. He'll simply tell the local paper that you never showed up at all. ★ *(Posted 5/11/2013)*

Presidents' City Inn, 845 Hancock Street, Quincy, Massachusetts, March 3–4, 2008

Dear KoWojahk283, I do thank you for your generous comments on my posts, among which I especially appreciated your suggestion that I hang out my own shingle. As you know, this is exactly how I began on my current career. I hung out the proverbial shingle re motivational speaking. First I was in investment banking, and then I did a little day-trading, and then I became a motivational speaker, after which, as you know, I began publishing some of these writings about hotels I have stayed in. It is fair to say that over the years of motivational speaking, I've had a real impact on the lives of many friends and coworkers through my counsel in such areas as professional life and love. I think my overarching theme, if I were called upon to reveal one, would be *You Can Do It*. I believe in a phrase like *You Can Do It*, I believe it is a phrase with an *energy emulsion*. We should all take the time to think back on where we have failed those close to us, and we should all try to imagine that special adviser and counselor who would be willing to sit down with us, give a light, friendly smack upside the head, and then tell us: *You Can Do It*. You can overcome these moments of horror. You can employ the *energy emulsion*. I, for example, remember some things that I said in elementary school, and the shudder of misery I experience during the reconsideration of these incidents is prolonged. *You Too Can Do It*, KoWojahk283. Having said this, I suspect that you, KoWojahk283, are going to be the one who complains that Presidents' City Inn of Quincy sports no possessive apostrophe in the name even though it does. And then you will type: *Hotel room not clean services bad [*sic*]*, as though this conveys the specifics of your dissatisfaction.

I can't say I enjoyed staying at the Presidents' City Inn, and I am reasonably certain that I heard prostitution happening in the stairwell outside the room, and I may also have heard prostitution in the room adjacent to mine, I just cannot be sure that a fee was exchanged, and when I am not sure, I don't include the relevant details in order not to expose myself legally. I could not yet present my reviewing credentials at the front desk, as I had not yet published a review, but I had a confirmation number, and I had paid in advance. At times it seemed as though the fellow at the front desk and I were not communicating in exactly the same tongue, and it is true that there was thick Plexiglas between this staff person and me while we had our discussion, and it is likewise true that he failed to make eye contact (one of the very basic requirements in my motivational-speaking class).

I quickly realized that the three-figure price I had paid through a third-party discounter was far in excess of what was warranted under the circumstances. Please note the high fence around the Presidents' City Inn, and the rather sinister men ambling around outside, and the sheets with cigarette holes in them, and Continental breakfast of white bread and bagels but an inoperable toaster and not so much as a little single-serving sleeve of grape jelly. I didn't sleep ten minutes while there and lived in fear of the possibility that this was not just a motel, this was a bad-luck bazaar, all poor decision-making and synthetic opiates, and while lying in bed in the Presidents' City Inn I understood that *L'accueil est deplorable la ventilation de la salle de bain fait autant de bruit qu un moteur d'avion*, which is you, KoWojahk283, breaking badly into another language, as you do on occasion in your comments. But just because I am not

76

willing to go as far as you in the language of outrage does not mean, despite your suggestion, that I am an employee of the hotel or motel about which I post my remarks.

In fact, I take umbrage, a little bit, at this suggestion. I am not an employee of any lodging establishment, and certainly not of the Presidents' City Inn, whose employees are probably mortuary students or compulsive masturbators or people from countries where the citizenry subsists on less than a dollar a day. I have never been an employee of the Presidents' City Inn, nor have I been an employee of any other motel, KoWojahk283. In order to operate free of conflict of interest as a reviewer, I never take any perquisites from any hotels, motels, or professional establishments, or at least I take no perquisites that are not available to the rank-and-file consumer (check for those online coupons, fellow hotel enthusiasts), and I will not be spoken to in this way. Please do not repeat your remarks that I have lost my edge, that I have grown soft from the months on the road, that I am middle-aged, as it is scarcely possible for a middle-aged person to have the kind of flexibility required to stay at a place like the Presidents' City Inn, to demand a refund after two or three hours, and then to go sleep in the car, because it is safer there.

It is true that some people imagine I invented you, that in order to be certain that the thread of comments below my posts are adequate to my purpose, I have found it necessary to imagine a first-generation Mongolian immigrant with a stent in his right coronary artery and a peanut allergy whose father was a tyrant, who votes like a pipe fitter from Indianapolis, and who is constantly trying to get women on this site to pay attention to him, and that I have done this simply in order to boost attention to my comments. On the contrary, I think it will be obvious to anyone who considers the facts for long enough that I could not dream up the likes of you, and your grisly English, and your outbursts of French, and your relentless talk about the private day school you once attended. I am not that creative. And therefore you must be real.

Before I lodge my rating of the dismal Presidents' City Hotel, let me say a few words about the ratings here on RateYourLodging.com. While I passionately believe in half-star increments (in a ★★★½ star rating, for example) where appropriate, RateYourLodging.com does not permit a half star, and this is a disappointment. Their argument is that if you're going to have half stars, why not have a ten-point rating system instead of a five-point rating system? And you can understand their rationale. Nevertheless, at times like these, when faced with rating the Presidents' City Hotel, you wish you did have a half star. Over time, and given a voluminous knowledge of reviews past on the RateYourLodging.com site, you will want, as I have, to split the hairs more and more finely, finding in the astute perception of basic services a will to critical refinement that requires more perfectly calibrated equipment, for which stars one through five seem ill-suited. ★ *(Posted 6/8/2013)*

Americas [*sic*] Best Value Inn, 150 West Dussel Drive, Maumee, Ohio, November 21–24, 2002

How the two of them slept, that formerly married couple at the center of some of my online work, is to be recorded today as a way of discussing what happened and how this married couple came to the period in which they no longer slept together at all. At first, they slept almost exclusively after lovemaking, though neither of them would, now, describe it as lovemaking; rather, they would choose a more clinical and neutral term so as to avoid seeming, in retrospect, intimate. They slept after lovemaking, because that is what one does after lovemaking, in the condition between waking and dreaming, and so, afterward, they were going from the one place to the other place, and they were *a tangle of limbs* (1). Isn't a tangle of limbs a glorious thing to behold? Don't you wish to be in a tangle of limbs? Ought it not be the case for those who have given up some of the hope required to continue with this charade that they should be offered the opportunity to go and see a tangle of limbs in a bed somewhere, or even a photograph of a tangle of limbs, postcard-size, in order that (some) hope may be restored? For example, the feminine head reclining on the masculine chest—is that not, in some cases, the most agreeable tangle of limbs? How about the position in which the feminine arm is carelessly thrown over the masculine face? Or where a pillow is mushed, to use the colloquial term, against a rib cage, and a head pressed deeply into the pillow, so that head rests partially upon rib? It is the carelessness of the tangle of limbs that provides an individual-size serving of hope, the absolute careless placement of limbs, involving some employment of the concept of akimbo, which word may be related to the Icelandic *kengboginn* ("bow-bent"), all while sleep takes place.

If the tangle of limbs (1) was the first of their approaches to sleeping together, the second approach was *rugged individualism* (2), in which they would begin the overnight in the tangle of limbs, thinking back on the very first tangle as though it were the greatest time, the greatest tangle, and they were not so distant from it. They would start out in this slightly nostalgic tangle, and then they would migrate to a position that somehow seemed more comfortable, because, after all, the blood flow in the arm was being occluded, and one of them did have a little back pain and needed to roll over onto a side, and, naturally, at first, rugged individualism meant facing each other, and perhaps kissing each other a few times before drifting off, and then maybe it didn't quite mean this, or the kissing part was forgotten, and there were a few words exchanged, a few kindnesses, and then they rolled away, and rolling away was so horrible at first, almost anyone would agree that rolling away is horrible, and yet it is a necessary thing, if you believe in the tenets of rugged individualism, because the first obligation of sleep is simply the sleeping part of it, but then the miracle of resilience is to be found in the fact that they came to find the rolling away somewhat acceptable, if solitary, and they rolled away, drifted off, sometimes pretty quickly, in their private dreams (some of these were nightmares).

After rugged individualism (2), there was the period of marital sleeping known as *staggered shifts* (3). Staggered shifts appeared at first to be a mere extension of personal preference, and who can quarrel with personal preference, which is one of the hallmarks of American life. If one of them wanted to go to bed well before the other one wanted to go to bed, who could object, because the day would come when they could retreat back to rugged individualism, it was right there waiting to be re-employed, and so staggered shifts should not be interpreted as some kind of loss, some kind of giving up. There were occasions during the period of staggered shifts when, out of the murk of semiconsciousness, they occasionally found themselves lovemaking, my God, so unsuspected and sweet, and it wasn't as if they had forgotten all that they knew about the adventure of meeting a new body and mapping its latitudes, its tastes. Suddenly, they were awake and alive, and they had cast off the staggered shifts, or perhaps triumphed over them, and they were goading each other on and it was good, and because they were lovemaking they went back, as through time, to the tangle of limbs.

Well, it's my duty to tell you that the middle-of-the-night lovemaking was on the temporary side, or rather the episodes of this old skill diminished, grew infrequent, and soon, it was not just that they went to bed at different times (3), it was that they also *awakened at different times* (3.5), and didn't even know that lovely pre- and postsomnolence fumbling that is a couple trying to brush its teeth and change in and out of the outfits of the day; all of this became something that they each did alone, while the other was either asleep or out in an adjacent room gazing catatonically at a television. And in this manner, the period of staggered shifts (3) in turn gave way to *haphephobia* (4)—one of those half-Latinate and half-Greek technical terms—wherein one of the two of them did not want to be touched by the other (and these roles occasionally shifted) and would recoil if touching was introduced. Sometimes this would be the simplest physical interaction of all—in trying to arrange a pillow, one of them briefly made contact. The recoiling was immediate in the eyes of the one touched, this touched party gazing vapidly as though the touching party, the grazing party, were a stranger, just someone that he or she might meet in an airport dining establishment; the look would linger, the gaze of strangers, in this stage of sleeping known as haphephobia, whereby intimates are reconstructed as strangers, and not the kind who are alluring but the kind who you go out of your way to avoid brushing against, as if the person you shared a bed with were one of those unfortunates with the eight soiled Target bags getting on the subway in August, drenched in perspiration and long past a last bath, and heading for the seat next to you. In this case, the look hovered there for a moment until you realized that in fact you were married to the person a few feet away, and you had been in love with him or her for years, or that is what you said, and having bestowed on him or her the gaze of haphephobia, you cycled through eleven kinds of discomfort which I do not have time to catalog now and went back to the business of trying to sleep.

Except that haphephobia (4) is followed in turn by the period of *clinically diagnosed somatic sleep disorders* (5), which clamor into the contested sleep space like some colony of metaphysical prairie dogs, chattering constantly, keeping you both from making any progress in trying to move backward toward the tangle of limbs or even rugged individualism. The clinically diagnosed somatic sleep disorders are acute at first, and chronic thereafter, and they take all your waking time to deal with, as well as much of your sleeping time, so that you are exactly in the obverse of the tangle of limbs (where lovemaking is the space between waking and sleep). Now, clinically diagnosed somatic sleep disorders are some never-ending demilitarized zone between the two great estates, waking and dreaming, and these clinically diagnosed somatic sleep disorders are incredibly lonely. Especially lonely are the hours between three and four ante meridiem when you are next to your spouse but instead of thinking about love you are thinking about particularly invasive cancers, like pancreatic cancer or inoperable brain cancer. (In fact, clinically diagnosed somatic sleep disorders are basically a wakefulness-promotion system that in turn generates thoughts of pancreatic cancer.)

Sometimes in this system, actual physical complaints, like the aforementioned back pain, are converted into obsessional patterns of wakefulness, wherein a minor complaint becomes a symptom of a major medical disorder—back pain a symptom of cirrhosis, or headache a sign of brain cancer—and these obsessional patterns of wakefulness generate the need, the next day, for *a convulsive nap* (6), which is one of the things you should never ever do, nap, at least not if you are trying to get back to the halcyon period of the tangle of limbs, because convulsive napping only makes the clinically diagnosed somatic sleep disorders worse, and the napping, because it comes over you like a paroxysm, must be solitary, is always solitary, and always somewhat embarrassing. It's almost like you don't sleep with the person in question, your spouse, at all, because you are never in the bed at the same time as he or she is in the bed; instead, you are struggling with and against the bed, with and against the idea of sleep, with and against the good things that are associated with sleep, and this can go on for years. You pass the spouse, whom you now think of as a reasonably good friend, in the interior spaces of your address without comment. You cannot even begin to describe the horror of the cycle that is clinically diagnosed somatic sleep disorders and convulsive napping because you have not had enough sleep to describe anything at all.

And this gives way, as you knew it must, to the medical diagnosis of *sleep apnea* (5.5), bestowed upon you by the practitioner of internal medicine. The diagnosis has to do with your weight, the practitioner of internal medicine cautions, or with your genetic chemistry, or with sheer chance, or with adenoids, and you may need to have your adenoids removed and your tonsils shorn away, and in the meantime, you simply need to wear this mask and be attached to this tank, which will, at regular intervals, keep you breathing. This condition is very similar to the *chronic snoring* (5.75) that your partner now exhibits, your friend who was once your tangle of limbs. One of you has chronic snoring, which is sort of a chthonic snoring, and that has to do with the uvula in most cases, and the other of you has sleep apnea, and so in the rare instances that you do inhabit a room at the same time, you mainly keep each other awake, so even if you weren't preoccupied with pancreatic cancer you would not sleep because of the near-death experiences, and that is how the two of you sleep now, with the mask and the tank. Even dogs will refuse to sleep in the room with you.

And now you are embarked on a weekend in Toledo, Ohio, for

the marriage of a niece, and you are going to stay in a hotel together in Maumee, because it's cheaper than Toledo, and isn't next
to a strip club, which is apparently the case with virtually every
hotel in Toledo. You are a couple who cycle between stages 5 and
6 on the marital sleep chart, not quite having gotten to the cessation of biological function (7), though this is a misnomer in some
senses, as certain somatic activities continue after the cessation of
biological function; for example, cessation of electrical activity in
the brain does not necessarily imply a *total* cessation. A heartbeat
may linger on.

In any event, being in the Americas [*sic*] Best Value Inn in
Maumee with your sleep-apnea mask and tank and your bite
guard (it inhibits the grinding and clenching) and your prescrip-
tion for habit-forming sleep medication and your spouse with
the chthonic snoring for the wedding of your niece when the two
of you were once a tangle of limbs is the closest to a cessation of
biological function that you can get on an overnight without actually being in a state of total cessation, and what could be more
tender than this? What is more tender than the recognition that
you have changed, that you have come to a point where you are
not what you once were? Your former state is now sandblasted,
as abraded as anything else could be by the ravages of time.
What is more tender than mutual recognition of failure? What
is more truthful than the acknowledgment that what was once
mutual is now solitary and atomized? What is more exact than
the distance between you now? What is more perceptible than
your awareness that you cannot do what you once so wanted to
do, namely, be in love? Why is the fact that sleep is closest to
death so much more factual when it is considered in the theater
of connubial relations? Who are the two of you? Where will you
go next? After Maumee? Why are you always staying at two-star

hotels? How are you going to get through this wedding? ★★
(Posted 7/13/2013)

The Davenport Hotel and Tower, 10 South Post Street, Spokane, Washington, April 4–7, 2011

We didn't know much about Spokane except, in a general way, how to pronounce *Spokane*. We didn't know about the waterfalls downtown, and the bridges. And we didn't know that Spokane is surrounded by arresting countryside. The Pacific Northwest stuff: conifers, skeins of fog, snow on the peaks. We arrived at the Davenport just a couple months after the Martin Luther King Day attempted bombing in Spokane, and so the Davenport Hotel was incredibly empty. The Davenport, it's accurate to say, is one of the most beautiful hotels in the Lower Forty-Eight. It may be one of the most beautiful hotels in the entire world. Were you to discount hotels that are constructed primarily to house sheikhs—hotels that will never house you or me—you would have to conclude that this was a truly remarkable place. There's gilded everything inside, and potted palms, but it's the ballrooms that are outrageous, and while we were staying there—Snowy Owl, as she was called on this trip, and I—you could just walk into these totally empty ball-rooms (because how often in Spokane were the ballrooms in use?) and gape at their magnificence.

What I'm really driving at here is that the Davenport is the hotel where Snowy Owl and I began to collect our sequence of films of Snowy Owl running and dancing in public places and in extremely long hotel corridors. The bliss of dancing in a long ho-tel corridor (not that I have done it anywhere near as many times as Snowy Owl has) is to be found in the fact that you know you are showing up on someone's camera somewhere. There is not a chance that at any moment you could be asked to discontinue it. There was a very long corridor in the Davenport, that is true, but it was nothing compared to its Hall of the Doges. I don't really know what a doge is, some kind of magistrate in Venice, perhaps, but I do know that the name has the right kind of seriousness about it, and when we opened the door to the Hall of the Doges, K. was unable not to dance across it. K. was a dancer as a young person, and she can still jump pretty high, and even though she has a few injuries of the sort that a person is liable to have when approaching true middle age, she just threw her jacket, a hoodie of some kind, on the floor of the entirely empty Hall of the Doges and began dancing into the center of the room, irrepressibly. Did I know yet that this moment would describe everything we were going to be, the kind of people who would find it important to dance in hotels and especially to dance in hotels when otherwise besieged by the worst of circumstances?

So, as I say, here it was, just a couple of months after some cretin in Spokane had left a backpack with wires sticking out of it by the parade route on Martin Luther King Day, and we were just visiting the city as I attended a conference on social media in the motivational-speaking world, and I was failing to make any headway at the plenary session, failing to get any speaking offers, but we were, despite all of this, dancing in the Hall of the Doges. How long would they allow us to rehearse this dance? I personally know enough about Terpsichore to understand that diagonals are the most exciting shapes in a dance, how the dance starts at the back corner and moves forward toward the audience along diagonals, and I was an audience of one, and K. started from the back corner, and we had had our hard times, which I don't need to enumerate here, but now we were here in the Hall of the Doges, and

Snowy Owl was coming from that corner, on a diagonal, just like in one of those spectacular ballets where there is a princess and a frog, there is the history of the German peoples, or someone is a swan, and there are a dozen fifteen-year-olds whose toes are all bleeding as they do their extraordinary leaps, and it was all exactly like that, and I was worried about security coming to tell us that our stay was terminated in this hotel that was too good for us, but I was also worried about the dance ending, worried about the time after the dance, when the moment that had brought it about would begin to slip away. ★★★★★ *(Posted 7/20/2013)*

The Mason Inn Conference Center and Hotel, 4352 Mason Pond Drive, George Mason University, Fairfax, Virginia, June 3–5, 2005

The question you want to ask about certain lodgings, even if they are newly constructed or newly renovated hotels primarily for alumni who happen to be visiting the campus, is whether sex in these hotels is somehow better than sex at home. There should be a way to test this, there should be a sex-related metric with which you could measure sex in hotels, especially the illicit variety, but of what would that metric consist? How about increments of remorse? Increments of remorse can be measured in hesitations of footfall. Increments of remorse are measured in *la nausée.* Are you more remorseful after sex at home or after sex at the hotel? Or are your orgasmic epiphanies more or less epiphanic? In certain women's magazines, it is always possible to speak of mind-blowing orgasms, but never do these magazines advertise diminished remorse. Have less sexual remorse with him at home! Or is it only the male of the species who feels incremental postorgasmic remorse?

You are not the one at the conference. You are the one staying behind in the hotel room, logging too many hours watching ESPN, simply waiting, just waiting, for the time when a certain language arts instructor (back during a brief recidivist spell after a years-long break) will come up to the room and torture you a little bit, because you have not very much going on, except that you have left someone at home, and because of the increments of remorse, a certain amount of ordering-in of foods, especially ice cream, has taken place, despite the fact that any ordered-in foods are going on the credit card of the language arts instructor. You are fat, you are indolent, you are middle-aged, and you are tenuously employed. You are in this newly constructed hotel, and you are looking out at the shiny newly constructed veneer on the campus of George Mason University and thinking that a great many of your very best days are behind you now, which means that you are emotionally affected by commercials for Cialis. You are hoping that the sexual torture that will eventually ensue from the language arts instructor will be noteworthy for varieties of torture not yet experienced so that you will be distracted and your shame will be temporarily mitigated and your increments of remorse will be temporarily diminished by the hotel and the sexual torture and the oblivion.

This is all as it should be, until the trip back to the airport and the dreaded parting from the side of the language arts instructor, when you will be released back into your life, and then where will be all the devices, the serrated metal objects, the ropes and binder clips and clothespins that were attached to you in an attempt to get your attention? You should be forced to wear the binder clips on your intimate parts back into your life, instead of confining all of this torture to the Mason Inn Conference Center and Hotel, which is actually squeaky clean and staffed by people who are of good humor, even though they are hosting a conference on the feminist art and literature of the seventies, a subject you know nothing about except what the language arts instructor tells you when she ties you up and threatens your life, vows to put out cigarettes on your inner thighs, and forces you to listen to incredibly long digests of the meals after conference events.

And then B. said that this was not a fair and equitable seating arrangement at the table, not if the department chair was going to sit at the head of the table. This was a revanchist seating arrangement. This was a seating arrangement that perpetuated certain self-hating stereotypes among people of color in the group, and really the best thing to do would be for all of them to stand around the table in a modular way, not in front of seats, but rather at some discreet distance from the seats, so that there would be an implicit reordering of seating customs, and so that the hierarchy of roles that left intact an unexamined privilege for white members of the delegation would be interrogated. That is, there would be no sitting down until they had had a discussion of these procrustean seating arrangements, a discussion that was feminine in the following way — indeterminate, nonlinear, unfixed, and nonteleological, but with syndicalist roots — until the group arrived, perhaps through some theoretical way, at a homosocial consensus, because anything short of homosocial consensus was a de facto reduplication of patriarchal structures, of neoliberal paternalist privilege, anything achieved through persuasion of a rigid sort was a replication of patriarchal structures, and even the shape of the table must be fit for negotiation, or at least under discussion, a biomorphic shape with negative space being preferable, because the fact that the restaurant had only a few circular tables and was more likely to push four-tops together to make sixteen meant that there would be an obelisk shape to the table, which was unacceptable, only a circular table would do, or perhaps an oval table, or, if there was enough discussion, perhaps a table that had a circle at one end and rectangular features at the other end, as long as the chair of the department was not at an end, because the point, the language arts instructor remarked, *was to avoid anything that was*

demonstrably phallic, because we were there to have an important depart-
mental meeting about which of the applicants we were likely to hire, and even
though one of the applicants was, alas, a guy, he was the guy who was giv-
ing the paper on Stein, and the woman applicant was giving hers on Joni
Mitchell post-1974, specifically the album called Hejira, *and of course all*
of us revere Joni Mitchell, but we just think she's not rigorous enough as a
discipline, and this is of course when the language arts instructor at-
taches a clothespin to a certain intimate part of you.

It's not the single most painful thing that ever happened
to you—that would be, let's see, the legal dissolution of your
marriage—but it's on the list. When you have several clothespins
attached to you and you are directed to go stand by the window
and watch the students marching across the quadrangle while you
are whipped on the posterior region with a leather belt, then
you begin, for a moment, to be distracted from increments of
shame, while, it should be said, adding more increments of shame
onto the total, so the entire experience—including the Mason
Inn Conference Center and Hotel, which you can barely remember except for the lobby and the bar and the kindliness of the
concierge—is about the arithmetic of shame, the diminishment
of shame by virtue of a certain amount of sexual torture, and
the aggregation of shame by virtue of a certain amount of sexual
torture, things placed in you in such a way as to magnify your
worthlessness, both releasing you from feelings of worthlessness
and increasing feelings of worthlessness. This is the basis on which
you might evaluate whether sex in the hotel setting is somehow
better than sex in a domestic setting. Does a preference for hotel
sex necessarily summon up the shame/worthlessness metric, or
does a preference for hotel sex lead to feelings of warmth and intimacy? Is the dilution of your marital bond, accomplished with a
language arts instructor who tells you that you are an abject slave

whose only purpose is to somehow keep the erogenous part of you going for another twenty-four hours, something to be proud of or something to be ashamed of, and is the oscillation between these thoughts enough to keep you alert at the Mason Inn Conference Center and Hotel during the long, tedious periods of ESPN watching? At least until the hour when she comes in and says, in fact, that she is no longer uncertain about moving on. ★★★★
(Posted 7/27/2013)

Sid's Hardware, 345 Jay Street, Brooklyn, New York, October 8–10, 2008

Once I knew this guy in real estate. I didn't contact the guy in real estate until my wife asked me to find a new address for myself, and then I contacted him. I asked if he knew anywhere I could stay for an extremely modest price while I figured out my next move. He said sure, I could stay in Sid's Hardware, which had recently relocated to Gowanus, leaving their space downtown empty. It was more square footage (something like three thousand square feet) than any apartment I had ever had. My friend was the kind of guy who would stress the square footage and the location (downtown, convenient to mass transit *and* family court). The storefront was opaque, so no one would be able to see in, and I would not be able to see out. I asked my friend, jokingly, if the location featured poltergeists, because if I was going to stay in there by myself for a few days, I needed to know about all the paranormal activity. He laughed, and then there was an awkward silence. For the three days that followed, all I could think about was the silence. Was he trying to tell me something?

There were two and a half floors in Sid's. The main floor was where the cash registers had been—this I knew because there was still a sign that said *Cash Registers* hanging from the ceiling. Adjacent and above, up some steps, there was a secured office space where Sid must have hidden himself, periodically taking time from the counting of profits to oversee what he imagined were the shifty and unprofessional cashiers. The office also housed the punch clock that had once been used to oppress the hourly indentured servants. This became apparent when, on the second night, I jimmied open the door to the office. The following were the other items remaining in Sid's Hardware, all three thousand square feet of it, during my brief residence: a ladder, two dusty throw pillows, a hot-water heater, a beat-up old cassette/radio/CD player, one trash bin, some toilet paper, a shovel, a few pieces of posterboard, some tacks, some blue electrical tape, one large bag (a cubic foot or so?) of mulch (pine bark), and, downstairs, several seriously outdated computer monitors and printers that obviously were more expensive to dispose of than to leave behind. I brought with me the following items: an air mattress, a sleeping bag, an inflatable pillow, a flashlight, some toiletries, a couple days' changes of clothes, and a suit. I had almost nothing else, nor would I, after the divorce agreement was completed.

My real estate friend, Brice, left Sid's open and a key just inside. He observed that no one on earth would want to break into Sid's, even though it was downtown near several large, cut-rate shoe emporia of the Fulton Mall neighborhood, and this was not exactly a statement that comforted me, when, on the eighth of October, my wife sent me a proposal for the division of property involving my surrender of enormous amounts of savings and items of nostalgic import. I traveled by train to the Jay Street location and arrived at Sid's fully believing that there could be persons of a heroin-addicted, Night Train–drinking, or paranoid-schizophrenic nature living in Sid's, having taken advantage of its recent neglect. Sid's could easily, from the exterior, have been a front for some kind of psyops outfit, or a street ministry for some splinter church, or perhaps a sub-rosa battalion from NYPD Internal Affairs, full of stalwart and idealistic young cops about to infiltrate a corrupt precinct in the Clinton Hill area.

My first impression of Sid's was that among the traces of failed capitalist endeavor were all the varieties of quiet. Commerce is never quiet. This is why casinos are the least quiet places of all. Sid's Hardware was quiet like few places. This despite the fact that several bus lines went past, and the subway traveled beneath it, and in the diurnal hours, there were a lot of people going to the office towers just down the block. Sid's Hardware was quiet. From the cash registers up front, you moved back into the main floor, which must have been heavily mirrored once and hung with a variety of home-renovation products, tools, grades of sandpaper in handsome packets, and kinds of PVC tubing. (I find PVC tubing uplifting.) Alas, the walls, which closed in on any resident of Sid's, no longer bore any trace of mercantile purpose. A tiny water closet by the elevator would have just barely permitted the morning-sickness crouch of certain cashiers who had been impregnated by the raging and wildly alcoholic night manager, Padraig, who came from County Mayo and had no papers. Padraig was also known to vomit up the Jameson's that he had drunk in the half-gallon size the night before at O'Lunney's, just around the corner. He was frequently unable to remember who had won at darts. Sid himself had type 1 diabetes and was in danger of losing both feet to poor circulation, and he often shot up his insulin in the water closet, and none of his employees knew of his problem because he felt it was undignified to describe his illness in public.

Some steps at the back of the first floor, past the tiny water closet by the elevator, led up into an inner sanctum just off the HVAC apparatus. The farther back I got into the empty and silent Sid's spaces, the farther I got from whatever there was about civilization that recommended civilization over its opposite; the inner sanctum was where Sid's offered safe passage into the wild and unpredictable, which happened to coincide with my defenestration from matrimony. Indeed, what was keeping me from running loose across state lines with a one-legged prostitute and some open containers, plotting embezzlement and get-rich-quick schemes, insider trading and arms dealing? The back door of Sid's, past the ducts and plumbing lines, exited, according to this argument, onto the loading dock of a fertilizer wholesaler in Lancaster, Pennsylvania, gateway to the Midwest, where some guys were plotting fell deeds and wearing hoods at night. These guys and their pals imprisoned women in basements across the region. At first I thought to put my air mattress in exactly this room because a little bit of poison inoculates, but I decided, instead, that I did not want to be on my way to Lancaster and its horse-and-buggy rigs and antigovernment spectacles. But in the end I set the air mattress out on the main floor, where the outlines of human bodies had somehow been drawn onto the walls with blue masking tape. The demolition crews must have done it, the guys looting Sid's of its everything-must-go items.

I found, the first night at Sid's, that I could not wear my own clothing. I found that in Sid's I needed to wear someone else's clothing, and so the next day, on the Fulton Mall, I bought some camouflage pants, a muscle T-shirt, and a faux-silk bathrobe, as well as a kind of sash that I wound into a turban, and I stripped down to the most naked possible version of Reginald Morse and gazed at myself in the convex mirror of Sid's water closet, noticing that, yes, there were five or ten pounds that had not been there a few years ago, that my nose seemed to have grown ceaselessly, that there were gossamer blood vessels summiting the ridge of my nose, and that I appeared to have, not full-fledged breasts, but some kind of sagging pectoral musculature. I looked like a child's seasonal confection in the middle of a bad melt; I couldn't have aroused myself in Sid's even if I had wanted to, though I could weep with abandon in the three-second reverb of that space so that the sound of weeping lasted long after its proximate cause. Indeed, weeping hung in the room after I covered my nakedness with the used clothing of the Salvation Army, wondering if there was a friend, beside my real estate friend, Brice, who was interested in where I was. Would you have wondered, regular posters on Rate My Lodging? Was it the case that my wife had made a horrible mistake by ordering me off the premises? Did she ever feel regret in her tiny, ginger, five-foot frame? Was it the case that the galaxy of our union was expanding in such a way that we, its constituent points of light, were now farther apart than we had ever been and were getting ever farther apart at an unimaginable velocity?

On the third day, I ventured into the elevator of Sid's and down into the basement, the quiet of which was matched with a soupy blackness, and as I penetrated into the blackness, I became less and less enamored of the light until the light was only a certain rectangle of door, scarcely ajar, across forty yards of cinder-block isolation. There was a whiff of musty stillness, as though a flood had once washed into those depths. I had recoiled as far as I could recoil under the circumstances, and I sat there for some hours trying to disassemble computer parts in the gloom, as though there could be a monetary purpose for doing so, and I might have stayed there with the computers had it not been that someone else rented Sid's, and so Brice had to come around and persuade me out.

I had taken to playing the jazz stations on the old radio/CD

player on the main floor, and first thing in the morning I listened to one particular expert opine on the variorum recordings of Charlie Parker, and when Brice came in, I was unsure if it was really Brice or if his yammering was, instead, the jazz expert's. Up and out of the basement I came, dusty and carrying a length of copper wire, which I would have believed was implanted in my brain had I stayed another day. Brice said, *What the fuck are you doing down here?* I said, *Dictating my memoirs.* Brice said, *Well, you gotta get out of here, because we just had someone sign a short-term lease.* I said, *Who?* Brice said, *You'll know soon enough.* I was released into these my travels, my permanent condition of travel, and there was no one now who could stop me. Three weeks later, I happened onto Jay Street, and my footsteps brought me inevitably back to the exterior of Sid's. It had been rented to a political campaign. ★★
(Posted 8/3/2013)

Cabinn City Hotel, Mitchellsgade 14, København, Denmark, August 24, 2012

The hotel room without a clock must be made to see the error of its ways. What is the purpose of the hotel room without a clock? Is it the same as the purpose of the clockless casino interior, where you are heedless of the days, attentive only to the harlot who keeps bringing you drinks? Have you ever had that experience in which you are walking in a big-box retailer that is exactly like every other big-box retailer, and while you feel you know exactly where you are, you also feel as though you don't know where you are at all, and suddenly all the racks of inexpensive Chinese-made garments conceal the exit, until you feel as if there is not an exit, and you have the illusion that you could circumambulate forever in the big-box retailer, never quite repeating? Have you ever felt that you didn't exactly know the way out and *panicked?* What would it cost this chain of inexpensive inns in the Low Countries to outfit each hotel room with a small, battery-powered clock?

Have you ever waked in the middle of the night in a hotel without a clock and felt the desolation of timelessness, of living outside time, of the purgatorial way station outside of time? Have you ever waked in such a condition and realized that you were in an endless stream of bad hotels and that though you might alight in some apartment—say, in the New York metro area—your life, in essence, had become a sequence of hotels, and that you had become this way because you were a top-ranked reviewer at an online hotel-reviewing organization with no job security, very little money, and uncertain prospects? Have you ever awakened in the middle of the night in a hotel without a clock where you had come straight from the airport, at dawn, having slept not more than an hour or two, smelling like the yeasty interior of the red-eye, to find that the hotel was significantly *flooded* because of days of heavy rain, and that when you manually pushed back the broken automatic door of the hotel you had to slosh through a lake in Reception, where there was a cheerful and blond Danish lady who waved at you and said something in Danish about (you presumed) the flood, until you mentioned that you didn't speak *dansk*, whereupon you strode gamely past, because your true love and life partner, named Tanager for this trip, was already in the room, having flown ahead of you, from Germany, where she had been consulting for a new media-business panel that you helped her get? Have you ever waked in this room with the fresh trauma still in mind, not a room, exactly, so much as a sort of adult-size changing table that looked like it folded down—two fold-down bunks, in fact, upper and lower, of which the lower also served as desk chair—with the sink directly adjacent, around which a moldy curtain could be drawn so as to provide modesty while you crouched over a toilet jammed into a corner by the shower to pass a bloody bowel movement before hosing yourself off with one of those handheld shower wands that therefore was capable of being sprayed fully around the room and that drained out onto the floor by the bed so that if you needed to shower while in bed, you really could have done so? Have you ever waked in such a hotel and wondered at the fact that you were paying money to be in this hotel?

You were somehow duped into paying Danish kroner to stay in this hotel although the lobby was flooded with inches of water, and your room for two, smaller even than your room at the Groucho Club, was exactly the size of a prison cell and whose only premium amenity was a moldy curtain, but otherwise the hotel was so like a prison as to be indistinguishable from a prison, and there was no clock. Have you ever been in such a room? Is it not the case that in your timelessness, your jet lag and clock-free feverishness, you imagined, for days after this experience, that you were seeing Cabinns everywhere, each with its complement of students and foreign travelers trying to pretend that the Cabinn was not happening, amazed that there could be so much degradation and that it could still be called a consumer-oriented business and not a reeducation facility? Was it possible that the Cabinn was not covered under the Geneva Conventions or under the United Nations Refugee Agency? Should you go directly to the København commune of Christiania to try to score some heroin after the Cabinn experience? Wouldn't you, if you were more than one night in that clockless interior, try to score some *smack* in Christiania? Is there any way that this clockless interior was humane? Is it not in the nature of all things to be time-based, so that in all things you felt the steady march of that dimension of our natures, the decay? Was it not yours to total up how much time was lost in each and every chapter of your life? Your every failure?

You were never going to get back the night you spent in the Cabinn. You were never going to get it back. At the end of your life, you would think back on the time wasted, and you would think it was really not right that you were unable to reclaim the night you spent in the Cabinn in Denmark, but you won't even be able to say definitively how many hours you spent in the Cabinn, because there was no clock there, and you forgot one of those little European adapter guys so that you could type up your recollections of the Cabinn, but that would have been hard anyway because the only plug was in the bathroom area, where the water spillage was enough that you would definitely have been electrocuted if you had tried to plug in any electrical appliance. You have no idea how long you were there, though it felt like it went on endlessly, and so you cannot even file some claim for the losses of that night. It was and now it's gone. ★ *(Posted 8/24/2013)*

Hyatt Regency Cleveland at the Arcade, 420 Superior Avenue East, Cleveland, Ohio, October 19–20, 2012

I have stayed in Omaha, and I have stayed in St. Louis, and I have stayed in Manchester, and I have stayed in Springfield (it almost doesn't matter which Springfield), and I have stayed in Sarasota, and I have stayed in Albany, and I have stayed in Providence, and I have stayed in New Brunswick, and I have stayed in Trenton, and I have stayed in Columbus, and I have stayed in Milwaukee, and I have stayed in Davenport, and I have stayed in Worcester, which may be the saddest American city I have ever stayed in, and I have stayed in Stamford, and I have stayed in New Haven, and I have stayed in Albuquerque, and I have stayed in Fort Worth, and I have stayed in Moscow (the one in Idaho), and I have stayed in Tacoma, and I have stayed in Denver, and I have stayed in Edina, and I have stayed in Rutland, and I have stayed in Lewiston, and I have stayed in Elko, Nevada. In each of these municipalities, you could feel these American cities grabbing you by the lapel and trying to remind you that they were not nearly as bad as they manifestly appeared out the window of either the hotel or the rented vehicle. And yet in no case was any American city as woebegone and desperate to change its story as Cleveland.

This particular trip was my third trip to Cleveland in a year, and perhaps it is simply that the people of Cleveland are in need of additional motivation. On this occasion, I was speaking to a church group in Shaker Heights on ideas of fitness. Prior to these three trips, despite being in my sixth decade, I had never been to Cleveland, notwithstanding my admiration for the hard-luck baseball team that hails from this locale. You would think, from its hard-luck veneer, that Cleveland wouldn't boast a good hotel, excepting, perhaps, some four-hundred-dollar-a-night thing lodged in a distant safe area accessible only by helicopter, which would make it possible for candidates for higher office to avoid the masses of inconveniently underpaid and underworked individuals downtown, but you would be wrong, because in the nineteenth century, Cleveland built this arcade, this marvelous cathedral of indoor space not unlike something you would see in Milano or Köln, and tried to fashion a downtown around it, and this arcade has now been largely gobbled up by a luxury hotel chain.

Few downtowns are as ghostly and despondent as the downtown in Cleveland. Well, there *are* some other dead downtowns.

Detroit, as is well known, is so crowded with the afterimages of failed capitalism that it is impossible to take a step there without the sharp in-breath of astonishment at how shattered destinies can be. It is also where I first met the woman who became my ex-wife. But Cleveland is bad, and that hall of fame, with its neon hagiographies about musicians, is far enough away from where you would ideally want pedestrians to circulate that it can do nothing to help. And so dust accumulates, and disenfranchisement festers, and not even a rat would bother to come by. The arcade that the Hyatt now occupies is no exception to this spree of desuetude, and were it not for the grandiosity of its initial conception, it would be just a footnote in the barely-holding-on narrative that is Cleveland. Indeed, the words that best describe the arcade and most of downtown Cleveland are the words *deferred maintenance*.

But that does not mean that it's not worth staying in the Hyatt Regency, which occupies the entire block of the arcade between Superior and Euclid. There's no way this hotel throws off an abundance of profit; it's so enormous, and each and every stall of the arcade, on the upper floors, is a room, and there are hundreds and hundreds of them, scarcely occupied, unless maybe there's a wedding taking place. Hey, wait! That's exactly right! There *was* a wedding taking place. Beneath the used-car-dealer-size American flag that hangs in the middle of the arcade, there was a slightly zaftig Midwestern girl showing a lot of back and a lot of cleavage, and a Midwestern guy with a shaved head, and there was a whole host of friends, not-exactly-beautiful girls in blue, circulating past the miserable post office and the shoe repair and the knitting-supply store and the travel agency, each of these enterprises the folly of someone loaded with antidepressants who didn't really need to make money but just liked to have a shoppe in a location with jaw-dropping woodwork and glass and gilded edges; yes, there was a wedding, and some canned violin through the loudspeakers, and a wedding cake standing at the top of the main staircase, a beautiful marble passage up from the ground floor to the second floor—you could walk forty-five persons across that staircase—and here were K. and I observing from the third-floor terrace, like marriage itself was a lower circle of hell than the one we occupied. We had learned about the wedding not from the groups of worried-looking couples entering the arcade just as we were, but from the stack of photocopies at check-in that indicated there was an event in the arcade and that some of us who had spent good money to come and stay at the Hyatt could instead expect music and unrestrained laughter from 6:30 to 11:30 p.m., and that if we were noise sensitive, they would attempt to accommodate us. So said the photocopied handout from the assistant manager, who had probably labored long and hard over the specific wording.

K. advised me that Cleveland had a thriving dance-music scene, as do all hard-luck Midwestern cities, and although I'm not even sure what that means, a thriving dance-music scene, I think it has something to do with very loud and very repetitive music being played near dawn for people who are on self-administered medication, and my anxiety upon reading the flyer at Reception was that there would be a lot of hallucinating people with purple hair vomiting and shouting about the Apocalypse as they ambled around the arcade, but it was not that kind of wedding. We went first to our room for a quick nap and found that we did have an extremely deluxe view of one of Cleveland's finest multistory parking facilities; our room was nice, that was the best you could say about it, and Meg, at Reception, was kind to put us here in the corner, facing the garage, far from the elevator and far from the wedding, so that we could sleep deeply on the memory-foam pillows, and the thing about our almost excellent room at the almost excellent Hyatt, with its absence of ice machines and its overreliance, decorating-wise, on tan, was that our room made us want to go wander in the arcade and try to get the attention of the Chinese guy who had the pan-Asian takeout place, who was probably just trying to hold out one more year. We hoped he would make us a spicy broccoli and bean curd something or other, but the arcade was closed off during the hours of the event, which the flyer at Reception did not properly refer to as the wedding between Jenny Gartz of Sandusky, Ohio, and William Blunt of Bloomington, Indiana. She had met the groom at a state school where she was studying social work while he was studying sports management. Since we could not go to the arcade, and since we certainly couldn't wander around downtown Cleveland, because there is no downtown Cleveland to wander around in, there was nothing to do but watch the wedding.

K. was dead set on trying to hurl a penny from the railing of floor three into the cake, which looked more hatbox and less cake from this distance and which had no figurines on top. There were no persons dressed in NASCAR racing uniforms, there were no vomiting-at-the-altar moments, there were no last-minute speeches about how Jenny really should have married Travis Ritter, the urologist who had given up his true love—comparative literature—in order to procure a more stable income for Jenny during their stormy two years in Columbus, when Jenny really did have a few lesbian experiences, before she met Billy at a sorority-reunion event at a golf-driving range in some forgettable town out in the exurban farmland. There was no self-lacerating speech from Travis *(I took my eyes off the ball, ladies and gentlemen, and I know it each and every night, Jenny, each and every night)*. It was not that kind of a wedding. Beyond the girls in blue, each of whom, we decided, might have bulk-e-mailed malicious gossip about us, given the opportunity, and the great-uncle in the bright orange ski jacket who apparently didn't get the memo about formal wear, it was just another wedding in a nineteenth-century architectural marvel in a city bleeding red ink during presidential-election season, which didn't stop K. from turning to me, at the railing of the third terrace, with a tear in her eye. ★★★ *(Posted 9/5/2013)*

Windmere Residence, Windmere Lane, Charlottesville, Virginia, December 3–5, 2002

My wife's great-aunt was a woman of great resources. She was four and a half feet tall and had osteoporosis of the severe kind, but her rapier wit was never in short supply, nor her recall of trivial facts from the lives of extended family members. A slightly raised eyebrow (which one would have just been able to see beneath the enormous spectacles) was a signifier of abrupt turns in her story-telling. I rarely missed a chance to visit with this great-aunt, even if visiting meant agreeing to a family reunion to be held in the Windmere Residence, the aunt's independent-living address.

It bears mentioning that the wife's family was already well organized around the opinion that I, Reginald Morse, was insufficiently job-locked. The older feminine members of the clan, all of them given to macramé and tiered desserts, liked to take me aside, banter, and then introduce the surgical lancet: *Why aren't you pursuing more conventional employment?* This proved to be the case again at the Windmere. After admiring the recordings of the big-band era played through a public-address system in one of the reception halls and claiming to be unable to hear anything but the highlights of any conversation, and after helping the excellent great-aunt back up to her heavily festooned chambers (she was fatigued and wanted to get to bed early), I let myself be the subject of harassing remarks by one or two relatives whose idea of a good time was televised dancing competitions. Let it be said that my particular talents were not effective in a conventional transnational corporate setting, this is undeniable, and indeed because of my natural desire to innovate, I was not terribly good at serving as an employee. In certain circles, however, these things would have been considered advantages.

Uncle Don wanted to talk with me about ice hockey and he seemed genuinely shocked when I did not know who was playing in my division, and after several times through this particular rondo, I excused myself and went directly back to the guest suite, leaving my wife in the Rosewood Room with her fifty-nine or so relatives, along with their epidemic of obesity and their belief that the fossils of pre-extinction-event cretaceous sauropods were sculpted a mere six thousand years ago. Upon arriving in the guest suite, I laid myself grimly upon a multiply quilted bed, all of its bedclothes synthetic, and, using a new lightning-fast Internet connection in the Windmere, I began to attempt conversation with a certain professional, as shown herewith:

ManilPhil91: hello you wanna go priv

RegRomantic: ?

ManilPhil91: add time by put in credit card mc and visa

RegRomantic: oldfolkshome in VA, wife downstairs talking to second cousins

ManilPhil91: hahahahahahaha you put in numbers

RegRomantic: one sec where are you

ManilPhil91: Manila

RegRomantic: you 18?

ManilPhil91: 21

RegRomantic: parents know?

ManilPhil91: thx for putting in numbers want to party with this boy toy now?

RegRomantic: just had enough bourbon to preserve a dead body for a week

ManilPhil91: have cam?

RegRomantic: you don't want to see me

ManilPhil91: i am real person you are too real persons should…

RegRomantic: saddlebags of middle-aged flesh

ManilPhil91: what is name?

RegRomantic: Stu

ManilPhil91: hahahahaha that is a funny name Stu what is your job

RegRomantic: what is your name

ManilPhil91: my name Maurice

RegRomantic: real name?

ManilPhil91: do you have cam? turn on cam?

RegRomantic: I am just another guy sweating out droplets of desperation and heartache in the 21st century, there is no reason to look.

ManilPhil91: same guy from yesterday?

RegRomantic: no

ManilPhil91: day before that?

RegRomantic: no

ManilPhil91: i like to see you bc i like to see if u turned on then i am too because one person turns on the other person and this is way of love

RegRomantic: what is the weather like?

ManilPhil91: typhoon come in and sweep everything away bodies wash out and all the trouble

RegRomantic: a poem?

ManilPhil91: do u like when it's rock hard

RegRomantic: Doesn't everybody?

ManilPhil91: hahahahaha u r funny what do you want me to wear

RegRomantic: taffeta ball gown and a string of pearls and very dark lipstick, perhaps something like African violet or black honey or midnight orchid, some kind of extremely stylish but sensible heel, not like a stiletto, but something more square, and maybe some kind of perfume, you know, something expensive that has an exotic animal part in it, adrenal gland of mongoose.

ManilPhil91: hahahahaha would definitely wear if i had but is mostly very tight underwears and short pants sexy

RegRomantic: I see.

ManilPhil91: i like men who is going take care and maybe we could meet up in usa and you fly me over we go to expensive clothing store and visit tourist attraction like world trade center excavation

RegRomantic: you want to come to the usa?

ManilPhil91: more opportunities not to get beat up and drag through street

RegRomantic: what do you do with your days?

ManilPhil91: u touching self?

RegRomantic: does not work without tadalafil

ManilPhil91: your time run out eleven more minutes will have to buy more minutes

RegRomantic: money is no object

ManilPhil91: i take class engineering at university in Manila to get degree want to study nuclear engineering very interested in thorium as different way to use nuclear energy almost waste-free not like uranium plutonium half-life decay ninety or one hundred years instead of 24,360 years opportunity with thorium for

Philippines energy independent rise up from economic backwardness become powerhouse in 21st century tired of western countries controlling Asia

RegRomantic: so sex work is your day job?

ManilPhil91: like to have sex with men and i get to do it online also talk with men who are sad and help them to feel better in western countries because then they pay for my education that i cannot afford also i go to clubs and listen to dance music and shake moneymaking parts with friends and not think about the western men or my family that has no money

RegRomantic: I find this story very moving.

ManilPhil91: one time a child i admit to friend from advanced physics class that i am attracted to my friend he tells everyone and no one ever talk to me in that class again except to call me karne ng baka so i just decide if no one will pay attention i will go make love to men and do my own homework as student of physics in order that i more brilliant than any other physics student of manila and especially more brilliant than men who like girls

RegRomantic: you have that barely sketched in mustache thing that young Asian men have?

ManilPhil91: thank you sir for buy more minutes i take test for to be in military thinking that i will be effective in study of intelligence because i speak tagalog language and spanish language and some of arab and french and know how to get man hard and to cry with joy during release in English and other languages can get man to give up state secrets if necessary at first they take me in military but then realize that i am karne ng baka but probably only i sleep with recruiter and then he tell others in military that i am karne ng baka even if he is too and now nowhere to go but engineering school or usa or to nightclubs of tourists while still beautiful

RegRomantic: When I was young I wanted to be a stock trader or a radical theologian, or I wanted to be some kind of cult-oriented psychoanalyst. But I never got around to these things. I am interested in neurobiology, and during my brief period with the department of defense, I studied hiring patterns in the military. (I definitely would have hired you.) I consider myself a keen student of human behavior, and so I have read widely in the theory of personality. Just so that you know: I prefer women.

ManilPhil91: u don't want this boy toy?

RegRomantic: I assume you are used to men signing on here and picking through the boys as though they are no better than shanks of beef and picking you or your friends based on your thumbnail without any feeling about how you might approach the task and what kind of human values you might bring to the table, but I am not like those other guys. I have genuine feeling about you and your predicament, don't need anything from you but just the conversation that we are having.

ManilPhil91: i have pride in job try to do a good job make men feel love whether they want mouth or ass or rock hard boy and it better for me if you want...boss watch video and men that do not achieve release make it harder for boy toy to get shifts

RegRomantic: I admire your work ethic. I feel lucky that I have gotten a chance to talk to a man who takes his job so seriously.

ManilPhil91: if you don't want body then i will talk about oak ridge laboratory and how full courage men who made first bomb were if only use thorium instead plutonium and uranium benefit industry and industrialist but not good for environment and especially not good for Asia and third world—

It went like this only a few more seconds in the earth-toned Windmere before my wife entered, and I engaged in that time-honored maneuver known as the rapid shutdown so that while what is on the computer screen is no longer visible, it does not, at the same time, seem to an observer coming upon the scene as if the closing of the computer is happening in any way but the routine way. There must be a formula or a differential whose purpose it might be to correctly identify the exact velocity that will appear to be a task-completion computer shutdown as opposed to a guilt-related computer shutdown (a complex-sexual-identity shutdown), though this formula or differential will fail to take into account the engagement or nonengagement of the wife in question, who was functionally disengaged from the likes of Reginald Edward Morse. By *functionally disengaged* it should be assumed that we mean physically disengaged, and by physically disengaged it should be assumed that we mean in a painful, isolating way.

While the casual reader of RateYourLodging.com could perhaps reasonably suppose that Morse's painful, isolating disengagement from his wife would *not* result in a desire for ManilPhil91, that casual reader would lack the tremendous psychological insight that more engaged readers of my reviews have come to possess over the period in which I have been publishing them. Which is to say that everybody has his moment of weakness, where a discussion of economic disenfranchisement and nuclear physics can create a grandiose sympathy for the plight of Asian sex workers— not a sexual desire, it should be said, for ManilPhil91, so much as a Byronesque pathos for sociopolitical disenfranchisement. Which is also to say that the loneliness of the hotel reviewer is sometimes so pervasive, so overpowering, that anyone at hand will do, and if you have to pay certain parties to be at hand, then so be it. And in this particular case, I might add, paying for company created a tuition windfall for a gifted scientist in training.

The wife, coming upon the scene, insisted that I go downstairs to the main floor of Windmere and take in the art exhibition, which displayed art by the various residents of Windmere. I agreed to this proposal. In fact, there was a docent, or at least an underutilized resident of Windmere, who took us through the exhibition and indicated that all the works were for sale. Naturally I picked up a price list. The work was mostly representational and consisted primarily of the flower arrangements of beginning painters and the occasional *nature morte*. There was also a great wealth of landscapes. A couple of surrealist paintings were also included, things that had clearly been produced by painters with dementia. All of this work suggested that in the waning days of life, a visual artist will become preoccupied with the acute observation of what *is*, with the actual appearance of things that will not be seen for much longer. Distortions in the field of what is are perhaps the signs that an elderly visual artist will not come back from the edge of the known world but will topple off into and abyss. I paid two hundred dollars for a painting of somebody's shih tzu and returned to the room, and while my wife showered she called from the interior of the shower about when we might reproduce. ★★★★ *(Posted 9/7/2013)*

Tall Corn Motel, 903 Burnett Avenue, Des Moines, Iowa, 50810, November 30–December 1, 2009

Dear WakeAndBake, I have been impressed with your deep research-related capabilities, with your mole-like ability, given the scanty biographical details that I have allowed through the screen, to track, e.g., my credit rating and the status of my auto loan. I admit, WakeAndBake, that I periodically check my credit rating too, because it has been a problem on occasion. When you posted the number of my credit rating, that most American of data points, in the comments section of one of my earlier reviews, I was unclear on the reason for this particular violation of my privacy, though I did find it faintly amusing when, with a sophomoric self-satisfaction, you noted that last summer my credit rating had gone up two months in a row. I recognize, WakeAndBake, that to others there is a certain dastardly charm to your violations of my person. And the same goes for GingerSnap and her insistence on cataloging all the letters to the editor I have written over the years to various publications, both in print and online, as well as my most embarrassing status updates. It is, in a way, moving to me that you would care enough to look into these subjects.

However, I take an entirely different view of your dragging my child into this forum. WakeAndBake, the fact that you would dare to write about my child in the comments section is perhaps the most transparent evidence yet that you are a brain-damaged hacky-sack enthusiast and revenge-porn addict who can get out of bed only for a little of the old sadistic fun. I do not know where you got the photograph of my child playing a rental cello. As I do not have the image in question on my desktop, I am a little stumped about where you managed to procure it. However, that is neither here nor there. When you, WakeAndBake, and your like-minded friends accuse me of parental negligence for having failed to mention my child in a review up to this point (and perhaps it's worth noting that I have hinted about my child on multiple occasions), it can't but make me want to break your metaphorical fingers one by one.

Since when is it an obligation for me, or for anyone else in the online reviewing community, to give some kind of inventory about my progeny? Is not my progeny my particular business? Should not my child be free of the guilt by association that is RateYourLodging.com? Exactly how many reviews is she meant to appear in so that you can continue to have your profane obsession with these little reviews that I have been writing these many months? If I do it once, is that enough, or will you then hound me for an additional three times in this calendar year, urging me to include further mentions of my child? Do you have a child, WakeAndBake? Do you have a child with GingerSnap? Have you ever met GingerSnap? Perhaps at one of those online community meet-ups where it turns out that everyone has a club foot and cannot follow the train of any conversation without interrupting to talk about films like *Galaxy Quest*?

Okay. Here, in my review of the Tall Corn Motel, I will mention my child to get you off my back, because the Tall Corn Motel is where I was served with the subpoena. I used my credit cards a few too many times, I suppose. Leaving the state, apparently, does not alter the course of your acrimonious separation. Nor does it alter the fact of the estrangement between father and child. But everything that comes into the world, WakeAndBake, whether it is the browned peeling wallpaper of the Tall Corn Motel, or the child wailing out by the Dodge Dart with the flat tire that someone is trying to change in the motor court, the child with the befouled diaper hanging between its legs, everything, and I mean everything, is put in our way so as to provide us with the opportunity to grow and learn.

By leaving out the child, I have left out paternal anguish about the child, it's true, but I have also allowed her to live her life unimpeded by representations of her; for example, I have left out her delightful singing repertoire, among which are sections of the musical theater canon, downloaded from her brain with such avidity that one song often will blend seamlessly into the next, each delivered at top speed, often introduced with a count-in—*Okay, I know you know this, one, two, three*—and off she will go with fragments of something by Rodgers and Hammerstein or Lerner and Loewe, occasionally performing at the same time her floppy musical theater dance. Here she goes, in that floral print dress that she will not take off because she believes that dress confers magical powers, flopping around the kitchen and reaching for the crumbling Toll House cookie on the edge of the kitchen table as though it were possible to sing the entirety of "The Hills Are Alive," do the floppy dance, and eat the cookie all at once, at least until the end of the first chorus, barely avoiding collision with the stools by the kitchen table, back where I lived with her mother, and, at the relevant moments, spilling a beachfront of crumbs from the Toll House cookie, and then off toward the sofa and the coffee table, flopping still—and you might suspect that a beatific grin is a requirement for the performance, but no, there is on the contrary a dead seriousness to her face, not a look of concentration, but one that seems to believe the preservation of our musical theater heritage is a solemn responsibility—stopping briefly at the coffee table to look over a magazine, there long enough to ascertain that it contains few if any princesses, and then back to the second chorus until the volume of cookie in the mouth prevents reasonable elocution, whereupon my wife gives in to anxiety about the choking hazard and says: Stop.

I can tell you that I was once turned back at the border of Dubai, where I was going to stay in one of those hotel casinos in order to give a lecture on retiring personal debt. Getting back on the plane was utterly humiliating and professionally devastating, but even that is nowhere near as bad as the feeling of human failure that I associate with the abridgment of my visitation with the child, owing to the enmities and vituperations of separation. Some of you will imagine that the great number of hotel reviews I write are due to some desire to avoid the child, but this could not be farther from the truth. Some of you, those readers more charitable than WakeAndBake, will imagine that I write the hotel reviews in order to produce an additional income stream to fund the child-support portion of my financial obligations, and this, while partially true, does not tell the entire story. Because it is also true that I travel in the way I travel to find a way to outrun not the child, but my feelings of human failure and disconsolation that are attendant upon my inability to see the child for a full 3.5 days per week. (My tendency to do badly when it comes to keeping up with rent and mortgages and so forth, you see, has at times had a concomitant bad effect on a complete itinerary of visitation with the child.) Sometimes this disconsolation leads to an address that is nearby the child, and sometimes far, far, far from the child, in a town, for instance, where the freight trains are keening past from dusk to dawn, and where one of the most American of interstates, the august I-80, intersects with one of the major north–south routes, I-35, and where there are just enough people to allow for a major drug subculture, some prostitution, some hog farms, feed corn, and libertarianism, along with the worst motels for three hundred miles in any direction.

I always say, when I am giving instruction in motivational speaking, that you should speak from the desire to heal the most broken part of yourself. You should speak from where you are most wounded, and out of the desire to heal that most hurt part of yourself. Which man among us is not, most of the time, possessed of the desire to curl himself into a fetal ball? That's the place that you start from. You start from the fetal ball, and you start with the sense that healing is good and that if you were some kind of totally omnipotent or omniscient being, you would shine down a lot of love on the guy in the fetal ball.

Now, imagine that you are saying that to yourself, you, the guy in the dingy motel in Des Moines who is opening the door and finding there a suited-up business type saying, *Is your name Reginald Morse?* To which you reply, *Yessir,* knowing even then that something awful is about to happen, wondering if it's too late to retract the *yessir* somehow and replace it with *Actually, I'm Don Smith, Agway regional sales manager,* but, no, it's too late, you have said *yessir,* and now the business type is saying, *You are served,* and never has there been a present-tense statement of fact that has seemed so present tense and so factual, yes, you are served, and the little bundle of papers now lying at your feet compels your appearance at a county courthouse in _____. Imagine you are an omnipotent being looking down on this guy and the bundle of papers at his feet. He has done so much wrong, he has tried so hard and failed so thoroughly, he has not loved when he had the chance to love, he has not lifted a finger, sometimes, for the people who needed some heavy lifting from him, he has not called his mother in weeks, even though his mother is still hale and living in a retirement community in Connecticut. (His sister, as his mother is fond of telling him, semiannually, calls regularly.) Yet is he not worthy of compassion? Is this not the place from which to begin speaking now? The Tall Corn Motel of Des Moines, Iowa? And is it not now apparent, WakeAndBake, why I might have preferred to leave the child out of all this?

I met a police officer at the Top Hat Lounge, across the street, to which I later repaired, and she was unwinding from her shift, and she told this story about the Tall Corn, how there was a sign on a bulletin board in the lobby of the Tall Corn saying *For a Good Time, Call...,* a sign so brazen, and the police officer and her undercover partner, whom she described as significantly resembling a child molester (but on the side of good), did call the number in question, and the child-molester partner managed to procure a meeting with

"Tamara" in the alley behind the Tall Corn. He then donned his *Thunderwear,* which was a special pair of briefs in which he could frontally install his heat, just about where his manly proboscis lay nested, because this is dangerous work and one must not overlook to include the heat, and he likewise donned a wire, as they say in substandard police-procedural television dramas, and off he went, on foot, to the alley, outfitted with *Thunderwear* and the proverbial *wire,* whereupon he began a colloquy with Tamara on a price for services. Various menu options were discussed, including oral for forty dollars, at which point (according to the police officer), the child-molester partner began berating the woman of the evening, the working girl, for giving herself away too inexpensively. *Don't you have any self-esteem? the partner said. Don't you think you're worth more than that? There's no one on this earth who should give away her dignity for that kind of a price, I don't care who you are or what hard times you have seen. Don't you have self-respect? Self-respect is worth more than forty dollars! And what can you buy with forty dollars anyway? You couldn't even get a decent winter coat for forty dollars, for when it gets cold like this. You couldn't even buy a decent dinner out and a bottle of wine!*

On he went, though this speech was not meant to be part of the buy-and-bust operation. And the working girl, Tamara, took issue with this lecture. She pointed out that the price was fixed by her pimp, and they had been in this business for a while, the pimp especially. He was a prostitution expert, and they (she and her pimp, who perhaps thought of himself more as a dispatcher) did not believe that this was an unusually low price at all but rather a competitive price in this market, which was somewhat glutted with working girls, owing to the regional drug boom. *Still,* the child molester said, totally off script, *I just don't think it's right,* and she said, *Well, you're free to pay more if that's what you want, but I'm not doing more than what I already agreed to,* and then they set off for the room in the Tall Corn;

that is, they headed from the alley around the corner to the room off the parking lot, which she had booked for several weeks (and thus the sign on the bulletin board), and the working girl said, *It's not so bad in here, really, and it doesn't smell, but don't take a bath, because last time I took a bath here I got fungus on my back.* The tenderness of this advisement—fungus on the back—was lost on no one.

Now, let it be said, the officer told me, that there was a code, audible upon the wire he had concealed about himself, that was the indication for the lady officer and her cohorts to swoop down and arrest the pitiable and kind working girl, Tamara, and that was when the child-molester officer said, *The tuna is in the can*, whereupon the swooping was to take place, and why the code was not *The snake is in the grass* or *The worm has turned* or *The fishing will be good*, I do not know, maybe the child molester just liked tuna. You have to admit it's a pretty great bit of code, and one wonders only how the child molester was able to speak his line in the context of procuring oral favors. Nevertheless, the child molester did say, *The tuna is in the can*, and they swooped in, and the working girl was set facedown on the pavement of the Tall Corn parking area, and her wrists were cuffed, and in this way yet another prostitute operating out of the Tall Corn was taken out of circulation for a couple of weeks, at least until yet another sweet young thing with a drug problem decided to make some easy money. Yes, all of this took place in the motel where I got my subpoena. ★ *(Posted 11/9/2013)*

Norse Motel, 1120 County Road 165, Story City, Iowa, December 6–11, 2009

You know what else can really distract you from your low circumstances? Hotel pornography. I haven't really had a chance to rate hotel porn on Rate Your Lodging, but I think it's a significant part of the hotel/motel experience. (However, before I begin, it's perhaps useful to speak of that disagreeable colloquialism, viz., the noun *porno,* as in "Last night I rented a porno," or "There were several good pornos on the television last night." *Porno* sounds like it's Esperanto, and, as everyone knows, the dream of an international language that is simple and easy to use and based on Romance languages is an infantile wish. Esperanto is like giving the world gruel out of a vacuum-packed sleeve instead of actual food. And *porno* does not describe the brutish need of sexually explicit video products, and so, in my ratings of hotel porn, I will exclusively use that abbreviation, *porn.* You will find no pornos here. No Esperanto.) Often, when traveling alone, I will walk into a room and feel an overpowering need to defile myself. Nothing says lonely like a brisk six or seven minutes with *Candy Store Vixens* and some giveaway lotion and a washcloth from the fungally rich motel bathroom, after which the contempt for self will be amplified to a level that is familiar, even comfortable. So hotel pornography is a useful service to have available in a motel, and it was generous of whatever sex addict originally came up with the idea. There *are* men who need to defile themselves in order to get on with their lives.

So now that we have agreed with the idea of hotel porn and with the importance of reviewing it, what kinds of features should be peculiar to hotel porn, to a clientele that is busy, hardworking, emotionally blunted, ashamed, and cost-conscious? Obviously, the price point for hotel porn should not be too high, should not rise, for instance, to 50 percent of overall lodging expenses, because that will drive off the customers, but it should also maximize the profit potential in what is essentially a compulsive activity. That is, demand for hotel porn among frequent users is inelastic. People who use it need to use it and are therefore willing to pay. Ordinarily, when you purchase pornography, there is a period of getting acquainted where you speed through the film for a few minutes, trying to find a model who is particularly attractive and who is being well employed, and in this getting-acquainted period you can afford to have a film that wastes some of your time, because the thrill of anticipation, when it comes to pornography, vastly exceeds the reward of pornography. And yet, in a hotel setting, narrative exposition is your enemy. The consumer is not going to be engaged with such a film at great length. Therefore, hotel pornography, somewhat uniquely, should have no exposition at all. A hotel or motel that continues to broadcast exposition-heavy pornography is liable to have an angry clientele on its hands, because no compulsive user of pornography in a small-town motel like the Norse Motel is going to sit still for a long dialogue in a doctor's office in which a bored twenty-one-year-old with a triple-D cup indicates that she might have dropped her insurance card down her brassiere.

Additionally, there is the question of exactly what kind of pornography to include on your two or three adult channels at your hotel. While there is the danger of driving off evangelical patrons by including any gay porn—*Locker Room Studs* or what have you—there is also the possibility that a significant portion of these evangelical patrons are themselves gay- or bi-curious and thus willing to have a line item on their bills that simply says *Video incidentals* and does not specifically indicate that it was two strapping young guys with dog tags and shaved chests going at it for hours. A certain range of tastes only enhances the opportunity to monetize the compulsivity of the hotel-pornography phenomenon.

Third, the filmed entertainment we're after here needs to contain the maximum number of ejaculatory moments, because while these ejaculatory moments are often coterminous with the orgasmic release of the user of the pornographic entertainment—thus shortening the amount of time the film is used—there is the chance, especially with the particularly addictive members of the clientele, that porn is going to be used two or even three times in a night, and therefore it should not risk wearing out its welcome. A given film should, rather, deliver the goods as many times as possible in ninety minutes so that one fee enables repeated viewings, especially when one is in the room alone drinking beer, thinking about the past, regretting, and trying to avoid calling old friends and weeping. Under these circumstances, the pornographic video should withstand frequent use without becoming dull or hackneyed.

A guy should be able to walk into the room with the knowledge that residing in this motor court constitutes an abundance of bad luck, a milestone of failure in his life, and he should be able to turn on the television, flip straight to the screen that indicates what networks are included here (NBC, ABC, CBS, PBS, CNN, HLN, FOX, MSNBC, HSN, SHO, HBO, MTV, MTV2, VH1, TLC, Syfy, THC), and he should be able to find the pay-per-view adult-entertainment channel, strip off his tie, and begin the investigation of his own loneliness that is to be revealed in *Candy Store Vixens,* a process which involves the same old self-pleasuring techniques that have worked since he first did this, let's say thirty-five years ago; it's almost impossible to stay awake while doing it now, and anyone who could see him doing it would be challenged to find pity or compassion in her heart; he can barely keep the thing from softening into a doughy and unresponsive blob, and not even the enormous and artificially enhanced breasts will help, or the little-girl cries of ecstasy, which he is worried about the next room overhearing; it barely works, or when it works, it works in such a meager way that scarcely does the moment of halfhearted pleasure streak across his limbic brain before he feels the surge of despond. This is the pornography of the modern motel, which is the pornography of disgust. It is at the heart of travel in America, and I for one try to do it just about every time I'm out on the road by myself. ★★ *(Posted 11/10/2013)*

Willows Motel, 3127 Route 22, Boston Corners, New York, December 1–3, 2012

Again, I have to address briefly the idea that I am not who I say I am, a line of argument fomented by KoWojahk283 and by TigerBooty!, but not exclusively by them. The argument goes that no one could possibly stay in the number of hotels and motels I have stayed in without being independently wealthy. According to this independently wealthy hypothesis, which is about as accurate as the theories brought up in the recent inquiry into my refusal to discuss my child, I cannot possibly be an effective or accurate reviewer of hotels and motels because I do not, in fact, have thrift as a motive. KoWojahk283 has tried to connect me, however tenuously, to the Libor scandal, the implication being that I am someone who has colluded in the fixing of international credit rates and who therefore needs to hide out in motels like the Willows of Boston Corners in order to avoid prosecution.

I can assure you that if I were still in high finance, I would rather serve out my time in a minimum-security facility that has a squash court, attempting to set up effective bookkeeping at the prison laundry and counseling the other prisoners with motivational tips, than stay two nights at the Willows Motel. The Willows has no squash court. In fact, it has one telephone, which is out on the parking lot by the ice machine, which ice machine no longer has any ice in it. KoWojahk283 alleges that I am employed by the Royal Bank of Scotland based on the fact that my name is Reginald, which he imagines to be a Scottish name, probably because he comes from Mongolia. Others got into the swing of it, and rapidly the notion took hold that I was not only at the Royal Bank of Scotland, but also ICAP, the interdealer brokerage firm in the UK, and, of course, the omnipresent Deutsche Bank, beloved of conspiracy theorists the world over. Yet none of these critics has had occasion to verify my claims by staying at any of the numerous hotels or motels that I have been writing about over the course of twenty-two months.

TigerBooty!, who I believe is a South Korean adherent of her local pop music (Gangnam style!), because I have found postings by her elsewhere on the subject, advances the alternative theory that I am in fact a teenage girl, which is interesting to me, not only because if I am a teenage girl, I have an astonishing vocabulary and range of knowledge such as the Libor scandal and the Iran-Contra scandal and many other scandals, but also because I believe myself to be a solidly middle-aged man with a bit of a weight problem and a receding hairline who knew nothing about teenage girls even in the period when he was a teenager himself. (I did, perhaps ironically, lose my virginity to a Korean girl, or a half-Korean girl, in her closet, and it was not a terribly comfortable way to lose one's virginity, though I confess that when she agreed to pursue this particular activity, after years, literally years, of refusing to do so, there was a moment when I felt something of the solar eclipse in me; I knew I was being transported to a new period in my life where I would be substantially changed, confident, worldly, different, where I would not have to carry around the self-consciousness of Reg, where I would know something about the human body and about the ultimate register of love that I had not known before, and at that moment sex had not been cheapened yet by overuse or drunkenness or some lack of enthusiasm for life, it was something heady and mysterious, and I was about to taste its delights, but unfortunately it didn't go so well, and I cannot say that in the immediate aftermath of human sexuality I took advantage of the intimate knowledge I had gained of the half-Korean girl to talk with her about her hopes and fears.) So, TigerBooty!, when you say I am a teenage girl, you reveal your own paradoxical ignorance of how teenage girls talk—American girls, at any rate—which I imagine is with emoticons. My theory is that the accuser almost always accuses the other of his or her own shortcomings. So it is that TigerBooty! must be a Korean girl recording herself on some instant videochat site singing along with the K-pop.

Yet another antagonist, called RedDawn301, who has posted a lot on this site hawking various mobile-home designs, accuses me of some kind of responsibility for the 2010 Deepwater Horizon spill. Again, in this case, it is said that I come to establishments such as the Willows Motel in order to avoid prosecution, rather than to review the motel for your edification. Now, interestingly, RedDawn301 is enthusiastic about oil drilling itself, believes passionately in it, in the Keystone XL pipeline, for example, but he still maintains that the executives of British Petroleum are all bisexual and German and that they have the capability of storing and cataloging people's thoughts. Somehow RedDawn301 considers me to be among the offending parties in this case, and, in part, he sees a pattern of excessive comfort in the hotels and motels I have reviewed on this site, though I say he has not yet stayed in the Willows Motel, or the Gateway Motel of Saratoga Springs, New York, or the Rest Inn of Tulsa, Oklahoma, or the Presidents' City

Inn of Quincy, Massachusetts. He responds by saying that I must be a government agent.

I can't dignify all of these ideas about me with reply, but I will say that in this digital world of widespread fraud, in which elderly women from rural Michigan claim to be steroid-enhanced weightlifting experts and the like, it is useful, on occasion, to advance the cause of belief simply for the sake of belief, because if not belief in this world, then what do we have? If not the action of belief, we have only the grinding disappointments. You could go on finding weaknesses in the pattern of my online reviews when really what you should be doing, KoWojahk283 and TigerBooty! and RedDawn301, is going out into the yard and staring up at the night sky, or meeting people and looking for the good in them. And while you are doing that, I will talk about the emergency-escape plan at the Willows Motel, which advises that you should first feel the door to see if it's hot and also that if there is a fire in the room, you should leave the room immediately. The escape plan for the main floor, and there is only a main floor here, is simply to exit into the parking lot. How often this is the case! How often our only exit is into the parking lot! And how often the parking lot empties onto the county road, where there are only package stores and full-service gas stations. If KoWojahk283 were right about me, would I be here? Feeling the door, making sure it's not hot, and then exiting into the parking lot? ★★ *(Posted 11/30/2013)*

Hotel Whitcomb, 1231 Market Street, San Francisco, California, December 17–18, 2012

It has a dungeon in the basement, and if you don't believe me, look it up. Right after the 1906 earthquake in San Francisco, the Hotel

Whitcomb, for a time, served as the seat of local government, other civic buildings having burned to the ground, and so a makeshift jail was installed. Ectoplasm, for the purposes of this hotel review, is defined as a paste excreted by spirit mediums during the course of intercessory activity and/or a kind of gelatinous epidermal layer covering over spirits so that they may interact with the physical world. Accordingly, it may be that any film of gelatinous paste in the Hotel Whitcomb is "palpable ectoplasm," owing to the hotel's having served as a jail. Or it may be that the Hotel Whitcomb is simply not being cleaned effectively.

RateYourLodging.com reader Harmonia 13 has had occasion to describe spirit-related magnetic energy. Such magnetic activity can be easily measured and dissipated with "divining materials" and also with fresh garlic or sage-burning. If the ectoplasm on the premises is caused by onsite incarceration during the last century, it almost certainly also commemorates a number of deaths in the Hotel Whitcomb, both incidental and intentional, including murders, suicides, and murder/suicides. People seemed, at one time, to favor jumping out the windows of the Hotel Whitcomb onto Market Street, a hotbed of stripping, gambling, opiates, vagrancy, and other varieties of nonspecific grunge. You might want to ask, you regular readers of the Rate Your Lodging site, what value does ectoplasm contribute to the overall rating of a hotel? Do you add stars for ectoplasm? Or do you eliminate stars? Have I, the reviewer, ever experienced ectoplasm? you might ask. Have I ever felt a glowing gelatinous presence in a half-lit room where a deceased person deceased? Would ectoplasm be considered an amenity? As I have said, I personally define an amenity as a specific and unexpected add-on to the hotel experience.

I remember staying at an inn in a certain southwestern state where there was an outdoor hot tub. I remember convincing an employee of the inn to join me in the hot tub, which featured a timer that triggered compressed jets of water. Normally, I am a little insecure about myself without a shirt on, as my days of being attractive are now behind me. However, on this occasion the amenity of the hot tub created feelings of well-being, which in turn eventually caused me to reach out for the employee of the inn and pull her close to me. Generally, the decision to pull close a hotel employee is a poor decision. Unless there is a presumption of collective will in the pulling close, it is extremely dim-witted, this decision, and sometimes even when there is a collective will, it is inadvisable. Were it not for the amenity in question and the feelings of well-being and the pierced navel of the attractive employee of the inn and her unusually colored tresses, I can say that I would probably have forgone the opportunity to reach across the expanse of chlorinated water in the hot tub and pull her close to me, unleashing further waves of so-called well-being, feelings that are attendant upon a sudden experience of moving-into-nearness that was, in the moments before, unanticipated. Say you are working three weeks as a personnel consultant at a community college in the Southwest, and your loneliness is suddenly punctured by the moving-into-nearness of a hotel employee in an outdoor hot tub above which, in the sky, Canis Minor is clearly visible. This is an amenity. Why does this moving-into-nearness involve such surges of well-being when other things—for example, cookies and cider, or even hitting it big on Powerball—pale by comparison?

What about towel warmers? Some people really like towel warmers, and I will admit that there is a moment after a shower when a towel warmer is a rather extraordinary thing. Other examples of an amenity might be on-staff astrologers, or free onsite e-book readers, or perhaps a barbershop on the premises, or peanut-butter-and-jelly sandwiches, crusts sundered, on the room-service menu. The Hotel Whitcomb did not have these sorts of amenities during my stay there with K., who berated me for taking a room there.

And what if the ghost on the premises resembles your own father? Now, astute readers of Reginald Edward Morse are aware that his father has been infrequently discussed in this canon of work, but let's say there were, at each floor's elevator disembarkation point, mirrors facing mirrors, and while waiting for the rather slow elevators, there was ample time for reflection, as it were, upon one's own appearance, or the appearance of one's loved ones, in these ample mirrors enveloping on all sides. I was having, on the night in question, one of those middle-of-the-night perambulations, insomnia-related, and heading past the elevators for the ice machine down the hall, when, upon hearing something that could easily have been picked up on extra-sensitive investigative recording equipment, I stopped, because it sounded as though there was a voice, or voices, coming from *behind* the mirrors, as if issuing from the reflections themselves. The sound, if I was going to characterize it, was like a barely stifled sob, or a series of barely stifled sobs, something alto, or perhaps falsetto, from the throat, not the chest or diaphragm, but the kind of heaving, asphyxiating sobs you associate with high grief. I stopped by the mirrors and, in so doing, felt myself lassoed into their complexity. In architectural and design circles, the mirrors-upon-mirrors gambit affords the illusion of scale, but I was distracted, in overhearing these ghostly sobs, by the way that mirrors eternally reflecting one another muddy the reflecting pool with their layers of philosophical and oneiric speculation, with ideas of the infinite, and infinite regress, as if, it would seem, any kind of reflection is to be had only in the beholding of the infinite.

While thinking about all of this, hefting my as yet unfilled ice bucket, I realized, at first casually, that I was seeing a man—a man besides myself, that is—in the systematized mirrors. He was wearing a suit of black three-piece serge with narrow lapels and a red tie, from sixty or seventy years ago, and a fedora, and I wondered, you know, because it was California, if this was itself a hotel amenity, as with those amusement-park rides in which an apparition appears in your gondola with you—would the serge-wearing fedora-sporting gentleman have been visible to anyone happening this way?—or if it was an apparition visible only to me. With sangfroid I thought of waking K. and asking her if she would come and look at the suited visitant, the mourner in the looking glass, but before I could take this on (and the wrath that would ensue for having awakened her), it occurred to me that this was not just any man, but *my own father*. I didn't know, at that time, if he was living or dead, and I had not had anything to do with him since well back in my early life, and he was a presence more in his absence than in any other way, and that was why, perhaps, I realized suddenly that the stifled sobs were my own and did not belong to the mourner, who, when gazed upon directly, vanished out of my sight. He had been perceptible only with the literary *sidelong glance,* this ghost who haunted the father (me) who was worried about being another father who abandons his daughter, another father who is insufficiently present in the life of his daughter (stifled sob). Is that an amenity?

At one time, the Hotel Whitcomb had the largest indoor parquet floor in the United States of America, which is the kind of thing your grandmother would have known. For jazz-age voluptuaries circa 1929, it was a "see and be seen" hotel. K. went looking for weaknesses, and there were, it's true, not one but two toothpaste caps stuck down the old-fashioned drain in the modestly sized basin in the bathroom. The mirrors, by the way, that appear everywhere in the Hotel Whitcomb are slightly yellowed. Is that a feature of the original 1910 design? Or a slightly later Art Deco renovation? The dog-eared pamphlet in the top drawer of the desk indicates that the Hotel Whitcomb has been renovated to keep up with the times, but as far as we could tell, no significant renovation had taken place in the past twenty or thirty years, with the possible exception of the "business center," which seemed, when we checked in, heavily populated with mobsters. Was one of these men my father? ★★★ *(Posted 12/14/2013)*

Hotel Francesco, Via Dell Arco Di San Calisto 20, Roma, Italia, May 20–22, 2004

A charming little hotel in a neighborhood right in the center of the old city, within easy walking distance of many well-known tourist destinations, the Hotel Francesco also happens to be the hotel where my child was conceived with the woman who used to be my wife. This was not a joyful coupling, but it was a momentous one, a coupling that took place after a year or more of disputing, arguing, relenting, agreeing, disagreeing, and agreeing again, and which took place with the technological application of thermometers, calendars, medical advisers, and so forth. We were successful on this, our first genuine attempt, which is remarkable because preliminary ambivalence seems to have had no effect on fertility. If your chronicler was not ready to be a father before embarking on the process, the presence of a child nevertheless conferred on him the right and just use of the term.

The hotel played almost no role in the fact of conception, excepting that it was the place we happened to be. The hotel is not to be blamed for the state of marital relations. There was a functioning Internet at the Francesco, which is named for the beloved saint who loved animals, and the functioning Internet was able to call up, after merely a few keystrokes, the kinds of images of unclothed women in tableaux of female slavery that will enable one who has given up on marital relations to reach the necessary preliminary condition for the miracle of conception, but I do not mean to speak of this amenity (the Internet), nor of the hotel and its proximity to tourist destinations, nor do I even mean to speak of Saint Francis. I mean to speak briefly of the laughter of the beloved.

The laughter of the beloved is such an excellence that it can bring about positive outcomes in 98 percent of imbroglios, even when these are the worst sorts of imbroglios. In the early days of a romance, especially a romance which for some brief moments is situated in Rome, the city of the suckling wolves, laughter is easy to come by, and all things that seemed gray and implacable suddenly yield to the light upon hearing this laughter. In the early days of romance, especially a romance that it is situated in Rome or Paris or Reykjavik or Florence, the laughable is anything on the exterior of the romantic dyad, and so a traffic jam, or an audit by the Internal Revenue Service, or entrapment in the elevator, these are all funny, because they are the world attempting to make itself present in the context of romance, when of course the world is not present at all, the world is some kind of picture postcard, and it is this state of affairs—how untouchable the lover is by the facts of the world—that causes the easy laughter of romance, and this must be what Dante was talking about when he first beheld Beatrice on the streets of Florence, while the Guelphs and Ghibellines were preparing to slaughter each other; even in the face of atrocity, there was still that giddy sense of impropriety and joyful laughter that comes from the presence of the beloved. This is not a seven-hour wait on the tarmac at an international airport, this is the presence of the beloved!

The only problem is that, after a time, the jokes of the beloved become familiar jokes. I notice in myself this sense that if a certain joke was reliable before with the beloved, it should be used again, because the improvising of jokes is so hard. Why shouldn't you be able to use the material again? And so a certain predictability comes to roost in the eaves of the romance. The jokes become sturdy bits of lore in the romance. It's easy to turn the pages of the book back somewhat, to find the old hilarity there, maybe a few low jokes about flatus or extreme intoxication. This is not such a bad time, the long middle section of your journey through marital humor, and many things of the daily sort can now be accomplished because you are not so preoccupied with how the world is just a backdrop for the glory of your romance. The middle is the longest time in any story, and therefore the time with the most desperation. Just as you settle in there, certain that nothing much is going to happen and believing that things can go on this way, you begin to notice that the laughter of the beloved has become increasingly rare. The laughter of the beloved has given way to a sort of wry smile that is frankly retrospective and seems to have a certain melancholy attached to it. Try as you might to bring about a few good moments of hilarity, you are unable to do so, and there's a desperate recognition in this. It was dangerous when it seemed as if the beloved would never stop laughing. But that doesn't mean you want the beloved to stop laughing altogether, and this unbearable poignancy starts to set in when you realize that you are unable to make the beloved laugh as you once did.

On a certain occasion you are out with another couple or two, at a dinner, and someone else in the assembled company causes the beloved to laugh. Internally you subject her laughter to some kind of laughter verifier; you evaluate whether the laughter caused in this case is genuine laughter occasioned by a moment that is legitimately funny in some way or whether it is simply social, a laughter of a kind that might take place at any dinner and therefore insincere, even if generous. But worst of all is how this peal of laughter, coming from her short, slender, blondish physique, has been coaxed forth by a guy with a harelip and a job doing something IT-related. The whole way home, you will think about this; on the subway, when there's not really anything to say because you are both so tired, you will think about how the beloved laughed for a guy in IT. About what? About beer-making or county fairs? And you cannot get the beloved to laugh at all, or there is a ghost of laughter, a little bit of laughter that mainly recalls a time when true laughter once existed, and you will lie awake wondering about the former laughter of the beloved, and all of this wonder and worry will give way eventually to the nonexistence of laughter in the beloved, and you will wonder if the nonexistence of laughter should be a cause for professional counseling.

It's not like you have that many problems. You can make decisions jointly, and you agree on some things, and you don't fight terribly much, but the beloved never laughs, and not because you have given up trying but just because you don't seem funny to her anymore. You are losing out, entirely, in the struggle to cause laughter, and because of it, the world, which was somehow kept at bay, becomes a thing that you can't escape. Things go wrong that you can no longer fix, and when you come to this realization, that problems have completely crowded out laughter, that the beloved is not going to laugh again, and that there is nothing you can do at all to cause the beloved to laugh, this is the moment at which you attempt to impregnate the beloved in a hotel in Rome, in a charming neighborhood near many tourist destinations of choice. ★★ *(Posted 1/11/2014)*

Days Inn, 1919 Highway 45 Bypass, Jackson, Tennessee, January 21–22, 2012

Although the bliss that I feel with K. in my life now is a significant kind of bliss, an ultraviolet bliss, a cohabitational bliss in the convenient and (relatively) inexpensive city of Yonkers, New York, it is not the case that we, K. and I, never have little moments of negotiation, and I am only being honest when I speak, for example, of the bed problem. The Days Inn, located not far from the Rotary Club of Jackson (where there is an annual luncheon on "salesmanship and the American way of life," with guest speakers), is not notable for the excellence of its beds, and I simply have nothing to say about it except that it reminds me of our bed problem. We are not alone in our bed problem. Beds can be a significant issue with couples. There should be a therapeutic resource for couples struggling with the bed issue. To be clear, K. has always had a problem with chemical smells of any kind. She uses the technical term— off-gassing—and comes from a line of people who can smell a gas that to most others would be odorless and who are badly changed by their encounters with such gases. Our initial plan in the bed department, then, ran aground on the shoals of off-gassing, because if you read the reviews of the memory-foam-style mattresses, you will see that there's a significant off-gassing component to the early phase of memory-foam ownership. And, you know, I always read the reviews. (I assume all of you who are right now reading this review of the Days Inn of Jackson, Tennessee, which cost $32.65 a night, the night we stayed there, are readers of reviews, and some of you read my reviews particularly because you know that I am one of the top reviewers on this site.)

So after reading the reviews of the memory-foam-style mattresses and determining that the off-gassing components, so often spoken of in these reviews, were contrary to our needs, we searched for and found an all-natural equivalent to memory foam, one that felt just like memory foam, or so the reviews said, but did not have the dreaded off-gassing issue, because it was made of natural materials. This all-natural equivalent, which we were going to house in our three-hundred-and-fifty-square-foot apartment in Yonkers, the site of our cohabitational bliss, which we managed to afford through strategic subletting and, on occasion, living in the car for a couple of weeks here and there, was going to take up a significant amount of space, but it was going to be where we slept, which was important for K. and myself, and so we ordered the all-natural equivalent, a significant expense, and when it arrived, we were at first full of joy about the all-natural queen-size memory-foam equivalent, a joy that lasted a couple of nights, because there was no off-gassing in the land of Reg and K., but then things started to go sour. Though we had not slept on true memory foam and therefore had no way to know, K. nevertheless could not help feeling that the all-natural equivalent was not as soft as genuine memory foam, and she argued that her sleep had been slightly disturbed over the nights we had possessed the all-natural equivalent. We thought long and hard, and we decided that even though there was a one-year warranty on the all-natural equivalent, we would not return it yet, because it had required significant man-hours to get the thing delivered and installed in the three-hundred-and-fifty-square-foot apartment in Yonkers, and we didn't want to have to go through the delivery process again (twice more, you know, because they would have to pick up the all-natural equivalent and then deliver another).

We determined instead that we would get a topper, which was not a word I knew until the moment that K. said, We should just get a memory-foam topper. A topper, you may know, is a thin mattress pad placed on top of the existing mattress and then affixed to it with a fitted sheet—less expensive than a mattress itself. When K. called the online mattress-ordering company, the sales adept she spoke to insisted that a memory-foam topper would not have the same off-gassing problem because it was, in fact, a thinner piece of memory foam and therefore featured fewer artificial compounds. Most people, he went on, ordered a one- or two-inch topper for their non-memory-foam-mattress product, and we should choose a height according to our needs.

But what were our needs, exactly? Our needs were to feel that a bed was a place of sanctuary, especially after the many ups and downs in the housing area that we had experienced, up to and including living in our car, and not because our parents were awful to us or because we were recovering from joyless marriages or what have you, but just because a bed is where a sense of shared purpose first takes root, and so we tried to evaluate our needs, in whispered urgencies, while the sales adept awaited us, and then of course he added that the two-inch memory-foam topper, while admittedly a bit pricier, was superior to the one-inch in terms of simulating the memory-foam experience, and so K. said, That's right, that's what we need, she said, we need to simulate the memory-foam experience, and so we charged it on our card. A week or ten days later, we had a two-inch memory-foam topper that did not off-gas significantly and that adequately simulated the memory-foam experience. I will say that when my child visited, which she began to do more regularly in those early days of the topper—that little gremlin of the interior spaces, who was happy, at least, that the space of visitation was an improvement over recent living conditions, *I love it, I love it!*—she immediately referred to the bed in question as the *bouncy bed* and exercised upon it in ways suggested by this sobriquet, such was the profundity of the two-inch memory-foam topper in terms of its luxury and enveloping qualities. To lay your head on the topper was like laying your head on the breast of your slightly soft librarian friend. It was like sinking into an acceptance of the afterlife.

The child loved the bouncy bed, but K., after sleeping on it for a couple of weeks, turned against it, thinking there was something almost swampy about the two inches of memory foam, which did not off-gas, it's true, but which were otherwise a little bit too much for her. I can vividly remember the day she called the online mattress-ordering company again and described her experience to a different sales adept, who was probably exactly as good as the other. The two inches, she said, were just an inch or so too much, and even though the all-natural equivalent was a bit too hard on its own, now the bed was a bit too soft. The sales adept gave us the bad news, which was that our topper could no longer be returned, though he would be happy to offer us the one-inch memory-foam topper, which was more reasonably priced, because it was only half the size. (To this point the bed-shopping experience had been in the mid–four figures, or way beyond what was feasible without advanced use of credit card debt.) Accordingly, we purchased the one-inch memory-foam topper and removed the two-inch to K.'s former apartment in Long Island City, Queens, now sublet to her cousin, which she was hanging on to in case it didn't work out with me, a fact that was understood without necessarily being acknowledged.

In due course, during which we reflected on our bedding experience so far, the one-inch memory-foam topper arrived, and we put it on the all-natural equivalent, and there were a couple of nights where K., like a cosmetic-surgery addict who is certain that this procedure has fixed all the problems, pronounced the one-inch memory-foam topper a profound success and claimed she was sleeping better than she had ever slept, although I could tell when K.'s praise of a certain thing was a ★★★ instead of a ★★★★ based on certain tonal features of her voice. She could say the exact same words—*Awesome! Now that's what I'm talking about!*—and yet if you listened carefully to the tone, you would definitely hear in the tone the ★★★ instead of the ★★★★. So some time passed, and maybe we were simply exhausted by the bed problem, but despite the clear ★★★, we both pretended, as one, that the one-inch memory-foam topper was adequate to our bedding needs, because that is the way that cohabitational bliss sometimes works. The child, when she visited, that blob of single-digit girl matter who made me a better person, had no idea that we had gone from a two-inch topper to a one-inch topper, and still referred to the bed as the *bouncy bed,* and had to be relieved of her *mud shoes,* on more than one occasion, before getting onto it.

More time passed, and then, as you knew would happen, K. began to complain about the all-natural equivalent with one-inch memory-foam topper and said that it sagged in the middle a little bit, and so I volunteered to sleep on the side that she said sagged a little bit, anything to prevent K. from sending back the all-natural equivalent mattress altogether, because I knew when she did so we would again have to face the off-gassing problem. Her solutions would no doubt include scenarios in which I would, e.g., wait until she was traveling for her job, which at this particular juncture was the job referred to in certain circles as *party planner,* though this was no permanent gig, and then put the memory-foam mattress in basement storage for a week to allow it to off-gas while she was away. Or she would sleep in the "foyer" (three hundred and fifty square feet, remember) or return to her apartment in Long Island City (where, you will recall, the two-inch memory-foam topper now resided) while the off-gassing took place, whereas I was in favor of intermediate solutions: for example, rotating the all-natural equivalent with one-inch memory-foam topper 180 degrees and seeing if the sag was still present in the same spot, which would suggest that the sag had somehow to do with the bed frame or box spring and not with the mattress itself. This we did. And for some days it seemed as though K. was trying to say that the situation was now a ★★★★ situation again, but I could tell, each day, that the rhetoric of contentment was getting scaled back, however slightly, to a ★★★, and as a result of her ★★★, I myself started to feel a little bit ★★★, though this is not my normal rating, and, as a motivational speaker, I need to be operating from a ★★★★ or even a ★★★★★ position if I'm going to be able to spread the word of self-confidence and positive messaging to the denizens of towns such as Jackson, Tennessee.

It was against the backdrop just described that I booked the room at the Days Inn. ★★★★ *(Posted 1/25/2014)*

Sleep Inn and Suites Tyler, 5555 South Donnybrook Avenue, Tyler, Texas, March 24–25, 2012

What the hell were those guys doing carrying plants around in their wheelbarrows at 7:00 a.m., and why were they yelling in Spanish? More like the Do Not Sleep Inn! I distinctly heard *cámaras,* or *ocultación,* unless that was a hypnopompic distortion brought on by the night before, about which more anon. Why the hell in Tyler,

Texas, anyhow? you ask. Well, I'll tell you why in Tyler, Texas. I had this idea that I might take my motivational-speaking business and give it a bit of sizzle, in order to create notoriety for my brand. And if you want to get real attention these days, you need a little religion, a little institutionalized ethical certainty, and I was thinking that perhaps I could get my foot in the door of that megachurch in Tyler, whose name is _____; the folks there agreed to take a meeting with us, with myself and my girl Friday, because we are attractive and presentable fellow travelers, well spoken, forward-thinking, and it was a pleasant meeting where they actually gave us lattes, which I wouldn't have thought was a _____ kind of beverage, expecting, as I was, something a little more utilitarian, perhaps in the traditional Styrofoam.

If it's useful, I can bullet some of the talking points of the meeting with the staff, which involved my describing the out-reach and on-point messaging associated with my brand and the way I had in the past been able to bring men, especially men, back to the theological fold, at least where pride in family was concerned. I noted too that I had on many occasions spoken on the subject of the pollution of the spirit (or so I told them), and how the spirit should not be polluted, and how I personally looked askance at, for instance, a latte, although the one I had in hand, I hastened to add, was tasting mighty good, and if a person of my particular credentials should be needed at the megachurch called _____, I would be happy to render services, especially in pastoral settings, in the one-on-one of listening and sharing, in which I felt waves of compassion for the suffering of others. I liked teen groups, I continued, and K., who smiled brightly and wore a used diamond ring we had bought at an antiques store so that we would not appear to be partisans of any kind of alternative lifestyle, would chime in often, repeating the end phrases of my most powerful assertions. If I said *positive outreach*, K. would also say *positive outreach*. The fellow we were meeting with was called Peterson, and we had a fine conversation with him, and if he had administered a polygraph test, I would have passed a polygraph test on any subject.

Unfortunately, Peterson then said, *Well, as it happens, we're going to call on the Albert family this evening, perhaps you'd like to come along.* In truth, I didn't expect, and never quite expect, to be taken seriously as a pastoral counselor. But in the end we allowed Peterson to herd us into in his Escalade. He liked a friendly face, he said, and I certainly had a friendly face. I was remarking, on the way to the Alberts, that I had often read certain works of theology when I was back at the state school, and even in the dusky light, out in one of the subdivisions of Tyler, which consisted of mansion upon unimpressively constructed mansion, I could see naked terror on K.'s face (in the backseat of the Escalade), but God help me, I could not stop talking as Peterson concentrated on the driving, and Melanie, his assistant (seated next to K.), checked stuff off in a handy ring binder. I kept talking and said that if God had designed the orchestra, then the cello was His greatest accomplishment, and a good singalong was the fastest persuader, and no man converted on an empty stomach, along with a few other choice morsels, all the while thinking it possible that Peterson and Melanie adhered to some kind of murderous Texas cult that only masqueraded as _____, or perhaps they were going to apply snakes and their snakebites to us, and how the hell had we gotten talked out of our rental Buick LaCrosse, why were we riding in Peterson's Escalade? But before I was able to complete this thought we pulled up at one of the neighborhood insta-mansions. And stepped out of the Escalade.

Soon the Alberts and K. and I were standing together by the

colonnaded antebellum front of the insta-mansion, exchanging in-
troductions. *This is my wife, Swallow,* I was saying, when Peterson got
the call, the fateful call, on his belt-mounted cellular phone. How
could I not have known it was a setup? *Lord in heaven, no!* he was
saying. *Are you certain? Where do you need me to be? Which hospital? I am
so sorry, awfully sorry, to hear what you are telling me, Bobby Joe, I'll be right
down there, blink of an eye!* Ringing off, Peterson gave Melanie a look
of such complexity—at once compassionate, studied, malevolent,
strategic, and irritable—that it was clear, at least to me, with Swallow now shivering against me, that we were about to be hung out
to dry. In a moment, the speech came: *Mr. Morse, I am so sorry to have
to do this to you! One of the prized members of our spiritual family has just
taken ill. That was his wife calling just now, and I'm going to have to hustle
down to the local hospital. As you can see, the Alberts are the finest family out
here in this particular subdivision, fine salt-of-the-earth people, and they are
expecting you, and you all should really feel free to visit together a little, and
I'm going to go on down to the hospital, and Melanie and I will be back in
forty-five or so for some fellowship with you all, and I'm just really darned
upset about what's happened.*

By the time I realized that Peterson and Melanie were already
back in the Escalade, I couldn't think what to do, frankly, except
to make sure I had a phone on my person in case we needed to
call for emergency services. In an instant, they were gone, and K.
and I were standing in a driveway in a gated community in Tyler,
Texas, in front of the insta-mansion getting ready to minister to
the Alberts, who comprised the following:

- The father, by the name of Tim, definitely potted upon arrival,
  carrying some travel mug that was filled, he said, with coffee,
  though his coffee seemed to have a pronounced sedative effect.
  He slurred, and used the hem of his bathrobe to wipe his lips

repeatedly. It was hard to understand much of what was said. Hydrocodone tablets mixed in with the libation?

- The mother, Allison, was a chatterbox paying little attention to the fact that her man looked like he might pass out at any moment. She was upbeat and natural in presentation, in a way that was almost certainly compensatory.

- The son, Stan, who had not been shaving long. Apparently, there was nothing in this world that interested him, especially not the visitors to the house. He said he spent most of the services at _____ texting the friends he'd met while playing massively multiplayer games. He admitted later that he had, as an apprentice hunter, just bagged his first kill.

- The daughter, Allyssa, Stan's younger sister, who was the darlingest, sweetest, most self-effacing kid, cheerful of affect and with bad skin. Somehow the Alberts had managed to protect her from the Albert legacy. Perhaps even Tim Albert had colluded in protecting her. According to legend, her first word, as an infant, was *marzipan*.

The interior of the Albert residence was furnished mostly with downmarket appurtenances of the kind you might get on layaway, and while this furniture did not have plastic covering, it was almost certainly the case that the Alberts had considered plastic covering. It was upon just such an unassuming sofa that we were invited to sit. Swallow slid in close. The Alberts gathered in around us, and I noticed with a certain interest how the boy, Stan, sat in his armchair with his legs crossed beneath him. All four looked at us warily, as if waiting for adversarial courtroom testimony. There was no one else who could start the conversation but myself. I alone was so deputized. *Where are you today?* I said to Tim. *Tell us, where are the Alberts today?*

Allyssa, the daughter, slipped out to the kitchen and returned carrying samples of the kind of cookie known as the Lorna Doone, a sleeve of which was presented entire on a florally adorned plastic plate. There the cookies sat, uneaten, each member of the Albert family gazing upon them even as Allyssa at last took up the plate and passed it.

I know what grief and loss are, I tried again, *and I have traveled over these many weeks bearing my burdens, not knowing for sure if I could go on. This is the way of the faith,* I said, *and it's our lot. We do not carry our burdens in silence, but we accept where we are, as we also accept that those around us can listen, can help us with our burdens. I know that I have often felt better when I have written about my particular sorrows, and I'm sure that Swallow would agree with this, as she has been with me every day that I have been out and about attempting to carry the message.* K. said, *Carry the message.*

I did not feel total conviction, alas, and that is probably why I soon found myself preoccupied with the Lorna Doones. I gorged myself on a good half dozen in rapid succession when they reached me. Indeed, Allyssa and I seemed to be the only ones consuming them. The cookies went back and forth between Allyssa and me for a couple of minutes, and then I watched Swallow slip one into the pocket of her windbreaker.

Tim, by way of reply, began: *I think your church is full of goddamned fornicators, and I'd love to be one of those fornicators, but I can't be shit, not a fornicator or any other goddamned thing, because I'm stuck here in this goddamned house with this goddamned mortgage, I can't even fucking move because of all the money I owe on this goddamned albatross of a house, and I'd like to be in your church full of fornicators maybe chasing around some teenage tail or whatnot—*

To which his wife said, *Please, Tim—*

I know goddamned well what I'm talking about. He's some goddamned

Yankee who turns up in the house supposed to be converting me to whatever pack of lies and he's probably a fornicator and a homosexual and a Democrat—

Daddy, please, said Allyssa, and then to me, *Mister, he can't help himself, he won't even remember he said any of this stuff by morning, and especially he won't remember anyhow that you were here. It's nothing personal, honest.*

Swallow said: *I won't sit here and have you talk to my husband like that.*

Religious nuts think they have all the answers, Tim said, slurring. *You all die alone, just like everybody else. Let's see if you all can figure out how to help me keep the family in this house when the bank people come along any day now, how about that? I'm not going to believe in any religious anything at all, and the thing I'm going to believe in is right here in my coffee cup. Cheers, fornicators.*

Maybe it would be good if we tried to pray right now, I said.

A fine idea, Mrs. Albert said. *I think so.*

And each member of the Albert family grasped a hand adjacent, and I grasped Swallow's hand, and then we were in a circle, except the last person to allow his hands to be grasped was Tim, who had to put down his travel mug, begrudgingly, and I said, *Heavenly Father, make as to shine down upon this family the Alberts in their time of need, and bless those who would help the Alberts, and see through their reluctance and their doubts into their hearts, and keep them in their home, and may large platters of food and plentiful viands appear on their table whenever they need, and may their health be good. Shine down Your face upon them, for You alone are all-powerful, amen.*

It is true, for those who have been wondering, that Swallow and I have a secret code, a semaphoric language of gestures, an emergency vocabulary that we practice when we want to convey to each other the need to vacate an address without actually speaking. We know that circumstances do arise. We plan ahead. At first, Swallow favored a grabbing of the earlobe. I believe it was the right earlobe. This gesture had the virtue of being highly visible because Swallow was in the habit of wearing nail polish, and thus I would notice the lacquered nails upon her earlobe. However, on what was, unbeknownst to me, the practice run, at a Rocco's Tacos in Orlando, Florida, Swallow performed the grabbing of the earlobe and made for the restroom, disappearing for what seemed like twenty minutes. I hadn't noticed the gesture. I was left talking to her freshman-year roommate for the duration, with no idea that Swallow was in fact now standing down the block by the Publix supermarket beside some Girl Scouts soliciting money for a blood bank. On another occasion, in Wilmington, North Carolina, I absently grabbed at my earlobe for some time before realizing that Swallow had disappeared out into a parking lot, where, it turned out, there had recently been arrests for pandering. And so in the end, we settled on tapping the ring finger of the left hand with the first two fingers of the right.

We had agreed on this procedure not long before the trip to Tyler, but we had not yet drilled. It was therefore risky to try it, but when I looked over at Swallow, she was tapping on her wedding-ring finger. How long had she been doing it? Five minutes? I did not know. I knew only that once she understood she had my attention, she got up and excused herself, and after Mrs. Albert pointed to the bathroom, Swallow shut herself in and turned on the exhaust fan. Improvising with great haste, I asked the Alberts if I could have a little tour, and then, while I was out in the backyard, as young Stan was showing me his 12-gauge, I wondered aloud where Swallow was and headed nervously back toward the restroom.

I knocked and, upon hearing no response, opened the door to the dawning realization that Swallow had made the gutsy move of going out through the Alberts' bathroom window, still ajar. The window in question was one of those small, side-cranking windows, so instead of moving up and down, it swung out to the left. It bears mentioning that on this day Swallow was wearing a calf-length dress with a flattering neckline. In this outfit, she had apparently gotten herself over the sill and out the first-floor window onto the Alberts' front lawn. At least she had left this insubstantial aperture open. Then it was up to me, with my bad knees and my lower-back pain, to climb onto the bathroom countertop and loft myself up through the window frame. Swallow had gently and quietly placed the screen in the shower stall to make my journey easier. I was nevertheless breathing heavily and feeling myocardially close to God as I lifted one leg out the Alberts' window and then tumbled out, colliding with their recycling bin and dislodging some empties. I dashed across the front lawn of the insta-mansion adjacent to the lonesome barking of a neighborhood hound, a coonhound, from the sound of it. I had not run so fast or so freely in many years. I texted Swallow as soon as I could, meeting up with her in an unimproved stand of trees where the next tackiness of insta-mansions would soon be built, once the derivatives market improved.

All we had to do was get a taxi back to the Buick LaCrosse, parked onsite at _____, and spirit it away without being seen. Swallow, in her churchy dress, waited for me in a Tortilla Flats just down the county road, and I snuck onto the property at _____, slipped the key into the ignition of the LaCrosse like a repo professional, and coasted down the hill in neutral, all before Peterson or his coven knew that I was gone. Unfortunately, we had not yet chosen a hotel. In Tortilla Flats, we quarreled about our choices, and Swallow nixed the Holiday Inn Express. Which brings me back around to my initial query: What were the Spanish language speakers doing up at dawn? ★★ *(Posted 2/8/2014)*

Sheraton Downtown St. Augustine, 2201 Beach Road, St. Augustine, Florida, February 14–15, 2014

Early check-in is always a crapshoot, but in a good hotel they try to work with you. At this address, we were party to a rigid and inflexible conversation with the manager about why he wouldn't accommodate us at the hour of 1:15 p.m. It should be noted that K.—known on this occasion as Chickadee—has a medical condition that makes it extremely inadvisable to entrap her in heated conversations. No conversation with K. of this type can conceivably be winnable without resort to Taser. Nevertheless, the manager, who, it should be said, had decided that check-in at his establishment was at 3:00 p.m. on the dot—notwithstanding the agitated group of twenty-odd stylish young Europeans who were probably in St. Augustine for SportsWearExpo 2014— repelled K.'s wish to investigate fully his managerial reasoning on the subject of early check-in. The discussion with this manager proceeded in an uncivil way, including Russian Federation–style doublespeak ("When I say the room is ready at three, I mean it is ready when I say it is ready, which is at three"), until K. snapped.

In her opening salvo, she accused the manager of looking at her like he wanted to murder her. Each side escalated. A simple managerial explanation would have sufficed. If the Sheraton Downtown St. Augustine wishes to have a decent relationship with its customers—despite its dangerously slippery bathrooms that must send a dozen seniors to the ER each year, and its paper-thin walls that make it easy to discern which of the high school athletes berthed next door is giving which of his teammates a blow job— this decent customer relationship is well within reach. Simply don't stamp up and down with smoke coming out of your ears saying, *This is my hotel! This is my hotel!* (To which, by the way, Chickadee replied: *Your family must be very proud!*) Just free up one of those rooms that you know are available after hours of sustained chambermaid activity, those rooms that are especially ready for the demanding customer. House the customer. That way the customer won't have to say, *Listen, friend, I am a nationally recognized hotel reviewer, and my laptop is open right now, and I am going to begin writing my review right now, while you are still bloviating.*

It is especially galling, Mr. Manager, when you say no room is ready, vehemently refuse service, and then free up a room six minutes later, implying that complaint is indeed effective and that you are a dissembler. Many readers insist that online reviewing is shallow, that the reviewers are vindictive, that their prose is bad, that they want for human feeling, that their physical isolation from the person they are attacking suggests that the worst possible instincts are liable to come to the surface in this online-reviewing process. I want to prove otherwise. It is true that Chickadee, on Valentine's Day (we had come down south for a day on the links, on a Pricelined package deal and through some barter that I had effected with a golf-pro acquaintance who needed to expand his client base), treated the manager to a few choice words and then had to go lie down (when our room was ready), indicating that her ovaries were about to explode. Our Sheraton Downtown St. Augustine experience was already soured, but we did feel somewhat ashamed of using our privilege to gain access to a room while elsewhere the SportsWearExpo 2014 attendees were killing time, waiting thirty minutes in the manager's queue. We felt ashamed enough, in fact, that I, as a preferred reviewer on the Rate Your Lodging website, wanted to send Devon Morrison, general manager, a little gift as an apology. I went online and located a trifle that might serve as an appropriate gift, an amiable five-pound jar of attractive Japanese bonbons highly recommended on one of the most esteemed shopping sites on the World Wide Web:

Haribo Sugar-Free Teddy Bears 3KG

First of all, for taste I would rate these a 5. So good. Soft, true-to-taste fruit flavors like the sugar variety…I was a happy camper. But not long after eating about twenty of these, all hell broke loose. I had a gastrointestinal experience like nothing I've ever imagined. Cramps, sweating, bloating beyond my worst nightmare. I've had food poisoning from some bad shellfish and that was almost like a skip in the park compared to what was going on inside me. Then came the, uh, flatulence. Heavens to Murgatroyd, the sounds, like trumpets calling the demons back to Hell…the stench, like 1,000 rotten corpses vomited. I couldn't stand to stay in one room for fear of succumbing to my own odors. But wait; there's more. What came out of me felt like someone tried to funnel Niagara Falls through a coffee straw. I swear my sphincters were screaming. It felt like my delicate starfish was a gaping maw projectile vomiting a torrential flood of toxic waste. 100% liquid. Flammable liquid. NAPALM. It was actually a bit humorous (for a nanosecond), as it was just beyond anything I could imagine possible. AND IT WENT ON FOR HOURS. I felt violated when it was over, which I think might have been sometime in the early morning of the next day. There was stuff coming out of me that I ate at my wedding in 2005. I had FIVE POUNDS of these innocent-looking delicious-tasting HELLBEARS so I told a friend about what happened to me, thinking it HAD to be some type of sensitivity I had to the sugar substitute, and in spite of my warnings and graphic descriptions, she decided to take her chances and take them off my hands. Silly woman. All of the same for her, and a phone call from her while on the toilet (because you kinda end up living in the bathroom for a spell) telling me she really wished she would have listened. I think she was crying. If you order these, best of luck to you. And please, don't post a video review during the aftershocks. Also, not sure why so many people assume I'm a man. I am a woman. We poop too. Of course, our poop sparkles and smells like a walk in a meadow of wildflowers.

Why does anyone argue that online reviewing cannot be of the highest caliber? (And let me stress that I didn't write the above lines, they are by an online-reviewing colleague, C. E. Torok.) In any event, after reading Ms. Torok's fine work, I made sure the general manager at the Sheraton Downtown St. Augustine was the recipient of this token of our esteem. ★ *(Posted 2/22/2014)*

The Inn at Harvard, 1201 Massachusetts Avenue, Cambridge, Massachusetts, March 6–7, 2013

I miss the child, I miss the child, every day I miss the child, I miss a certain way that the child says things, the er-um stammer that seems to precede her significant utterances, I miss a certain range of the child's voice, especially when the child is singing, I miss even the child's incessant repetition of the "Do-Re-Mi" song, I miss the child, I miss the tangles in her hair, I miss the wear and tear on the knees of her jeans, I miss how the child insists that her pants are not jeans but jeggings, I miss even the child's numberless requests to watch television, I miss the child's spitting out of apple skin, should there happen to be one last speck of apple skin among the slices of apple provided, I miss the child at the moment she wants to be hugged and at the moment after she wants to be hugged, I miss the child's naked, enthusiastic sprints through our tiny apartment before she takes a bath, I miss the child hanging upside down, I miss the child reciting plot points in superhero books, I miss the child, and I experience missing the child as a kind of physical lack, as though I have not eaten properly, have not ingested a sufficiency of calories, I miss the child when she skips to try to keep up with the pace of adults walking, I miss the child when she (still) demands to be picked up, I miss the child and the way she eats string cheese horizontally, some days I miss even a tantrum by the child, I miss her falling on the floor and shouting as she intones the words *You are the worst father ever,* or the bizarre request that she never be called by her name again, I miss the child on sunny days and on days when it is too cold to go outside, I miss the ceaseless chatter that characterizes the child while in a swing, *Three little maids who all unwary come from a lady's seminary,* I miss being able to hear her, from the other room, screech at the television set, I miss the child, I miss the child's smell, I miss the child's insistence on wearing all the time that pink nightgown, now in shreds, I miss seeing the child in bed with the nightgown wrenched around half backward, I miss her waking me up to say, *Is it time yet?,* I miss the child refusing to go to bed, saying that she isn't tired, she isn't tired, right before collapsing into total exhaustion, I miss even the irritating hours of time that have slipped out of my human life span when all I was doing was trying to persuade the child that it was time to go to sleep, I miss the child, I miss when she says she is scared, so scared, even though nothing particularly scary has happened on the television or in the book, and how this requires me to say that I will protect her, even though I know there are some ways in which I cannot protect her.

I have not protected her from the fact that her mother and I are no longer together, and as I also have parents who ended their marriage, I am in a very good position to know that I have not protected the child, I rue my failures, yet I miss claiming that I will protect her, even though I feel the vacuity of this claim and understand the ways in which I have failed to protect her, I miss even the profoundly boring moments of being in her company, moments when respiration seems like activity enough, moments when the task is repetition, repetition, repetition, coloring in one more line, I miss even the princesses, I miss all the talk of princesses, I miss making up stories about princesses, for example, a story about Snow White, Sleeping Beauty, and Cinderella all having a dinner party and getting snowed in and needing the princes to fetch the carriages so that they, the princesses, will not need to walk in the snow, after which the princes bring snowblowers and blow off the sidewalk, and the prince who does the best job of plowing out the driveway gets to take home the comeliest of the princesses, who happens to be the princess called Snow White, I miss the child's proclamations about wanting to dye her hair black like Snow White, I miss the subtle gradations of consciousness, the emerging into consciousness that is the child, I miss the subtle emanations of a vanishing self-centeredness as the child begins to understand the world around her, and, nevertheless, I miss the child's demanding to have another birthday present, I miss the child saying that she never gets a present, even though my guilt about the facts of the child's life and my inability to protect her from the slings and arrows lead me to give her presents with some frequency, I miss the child's eyes, which are the color of flagstone, a better and more superior flagstone than the color of my own eyes, I miss the child's blond highlights, I miss the earlier, ghostly presences in the child of now, though this child of now will be a ghostly manifestation in some future iteration, I both do and do not miss all the manhandling of diapers and so on, but miss especially the growth that has made those things no longer part of my life, I miss the moment when the child tumbled out of her mother, and I miss being joyous about family as I was in that moment, which means that I miss what I once gave the child but can give her no more, I miss the child past and the child present and I miss the moments that I will miss of her in the future, I miss listening to the child breathe, I miss listening to the child cough in the moments when she coughs, I miss the child's detailed descriptions of her own waste production, her distinguishing of one kind of waste production from another, her requests for company while producing waste, I miss the child's remarks about her friends, which are almost always contradictory and paradoxical, *I love Mark he is my best friend even though he doesn't want to play with me,* I miss the child's vulnerability, and I miss the steely invincible times of the child, when her very resilience proves how broken and lost I am sometimes, and how what I struggle with, the loss of the child, proves that I am less able to withstand the slings and arrows of being than the child is, which means, in some way, that there is more that she can do for me, by schooling me in resilience, than I can do for her, I miss the child's sneakers, which are a size too large as I write these lines but will not be six months from now, I miss the way she used to apply the Velcro fasteners on the sneakers, as she often did before she began the process of mastering the tying of her shoes, I miss the spot behind the child's ear that I often remind her to wash carefully, I miss the area of her cheeks that is somewhat windburned by the gusts of January and February, I miss her sweaters, I miss her coats, I miss her socks, I miss her books, I miss her sleep friends, whom she now disdains, I miss the times with her and I rue the times without her, and I especially regret the times without her that are caused by my going on the road, and so as I go on the road and attempt to conduct business and stay, for example, in Cambridge, Massachusetts, right near a university of some note, I ask myself, Who gives a shit about Harvard, who gives a shit about the sullen client-services professional at the front desk, who cares about the Hamworthy design of the toilet at the Inn at Harvard, who cares about the view of the English Department out the window, who cares about the crowded bars of Cambridge, with their flocks of the best and the brightest, who cares about any of this when there is the absence of the child? ★★★ *(Posted 3/1/2014)*

Masseria Salinola, Strada Provinciale 29, KM 1, 5, Contrada Salinola, Ostuni, Italia, July 1–16, 2000

Things can go wrong during your vacation. For example, you could suffer a detached retina, which is a very serious condition and requires surgery. It is also possible that during your vacation, upon boarding the cruise liner or while changing planes in Geneva, you could begin to exhibit the symptoms of a bleeding ulcer, resulting in a sudden drop in blood pressure. (I believe there are hemoglobin issues as well, due to the acute decrease in blood volume secondary to a massive upper-GI bleed, or that is my understanding, though I am not a medical professional.) And sometimes people have little strokes; you know, not terribly complex strokes, but just little strokes where they have temporary aphasia and can't repeat numbers in the correct order. You could experience one of these very disturbing phenomena on your vacation. This could be your fate. (Or, as I have related elsewhere, your passport could be lifted from your pocket by Carpathian-speaking youths.) It is impossible to plan for all these difficulties. Why not stay home? But if instead of staying home, you insist on going on vacation, then this entry, about *agroturismo* in Italia, is for you.

In 1999, I was helping to conduct wine-tasting classes for a friend who had organized a number of trips in which foreign travel and wine-tasting went together, and I agreed to go along and serve as a wine expert, though I am not a wine expert. At first I thought it was going to be in Tuscany, and for months I went around saying I was going to Tuscany, and then it turned out that it was not Tuscany at all, but Puglia, which I believe was Mussolini's homeland. Puglia is not exactly cosmopolitan Europe—there are not cutting-edge runway shows there—but it is attractive in a Pleistocene sort of way. Puglia eliminated malaria only recently, you know, and basically what it does is produce olives and olive oil and a few other things, orecchiette, very good mozzarella, etc., and so the farms of Puglia established this *agroturismo* in order to try to create a market for tourists in the region.

The idea was simple: You go and live on a working farm for a few days, and you get to sample the wares of the farm, in the process learning how cultivation and animal husbandry are practiced in another part of the world. I know that some of you are probably thinking about farms in the United States and imagining traveling to that farm in Iowa that has a toxic sludge lake of pig waste that's several miles long, where the sounds of pigs having their testicles cut off ring abundantly through the air each spring. I had the same kinds of thoughts about this trip but they were unwarranted. It was not as bad as all that! The farms in Italy are a great deal more attractive. What were those flowers that lined the road? They were like frangipani or bougainvillea, some miracle that bloomed everywhere in the still silent countryside of Italian cultivation. I'd brought my wife, because how often did one get a free trip to Italy, and they were willing to cover my wife and two weeks in Italy, and while I would not get paid, I would get the trip. I needed the money, and yet it was the free trip with which I won over my wife. Ostuni, the town nearby, is called the "White City" because it is all bleached and Mediterranean. It could have been built at any time, the alleys empty and cobblestoned, and you could feel the moisture from the sea, the centuries of occupation in Puglia, the way its fortunes had twisted and turned with a range of imperial masters, the Cyrillic on the buildings here and there. Who would not have wanted to take a crack at Puglia?

At last we arrived at the farm, which dated back to the seventeenth century, or at least that was what we gathered from the sparse literature available in English and the gesturing of the rather truculent proprietor. He had a sort of Ernest Borgnine rubberiness to his face, but without the mugging and grinning. He answered yes to each and every question, even those questions that manifestly required answers in the negative, and if you tried to trip him up by asking him a question and its obverse in rapid succession, he would say yes to each anyhow and then quickly slip away before you bore down. At a certain hour in the morning, he and his brothers, or so we presumed the other men to be, would set off for the olive groves with their tractor and be gone for the day, though I never saw any olives being brought back later. Sometimes it felt as though we were staying on an olive-grove film set rather than in an actual olive grove.

Did I mention that the farm was a ruin? I'm going to say that the last wholesale renovation was probably during the early nineteenth century, before Italy was unified. There were a number of small, nearly windowless cells in which we were meant to conduct our wine-tasting classes, always at the end of narrow corridors to which you arrived via winding staircases, and in all of these rooms, cracks in the stonework overspilled with moisture and, one assumes, a bounteous harvest of mold. There was also a chapel at one end of the courtyard, which no one visited at all, and which was haunted. We were told by our guide that there were some bones underneath the chapel, though whose bones they were was never made clear. Inside the courtyard, the grass and scrub had been allowed to grow up without restraint, in a way that demonstrated the neglect like almost nothing else, and yet in the centermost courtyard, the sanctum sanctorum, there was a birdcage, which, despite the general disorder and lassitude of the place, was always inhabited by a pair of partridges, or pheasants, clucking and pecking at the tin floor beneath them.

No one but our group of wine-tasting Americans seemed to be staying at the farm, and so there were two tables at dinner, which was always outdoors, under the stars, and one table was the *famiglia* and the other table was the Americans. The dinners were at least three hours long every night and came with endless amounts of wine. There was always an antipasto, a pasta course, a second pasta course, a meat course, a salad course, and dessert. I was usually ready to go to bed after the antipasto. The wine tasters—mostly fine upstanding citizens of suburbs of the United States with a generous capacity for European pretenses, people who went to the ballet, or wore berets, or had children who were experts on Jane Austen—were ready to drink some wine, and even though Italian wine is not known to be as culturally exacting as French wine, it was all part of this experience for them, the wine, the food, the fragrance of the Adriatic, the fresh olives of a sort you have never tasted in your life. They would all hit the wine hard, and it did not take long into the two weeks we all spent together for certain marriages that had seemed rock-solid at the outset, like that of Brenda and Dave McAllister, a couple from Indianapolis who had been to Italy together three times, to unravel. It became clear that Dave's inability to let his wife finish a sentence had taken a real toll on her, and Brenda rolled her eyes at him the more drunk he got, and once, barely out of earshot, she made a joke about asphyxiating him.

Only a few nights elapsed before I was leaving dinner early with the excuse of preparing the next day's lecture and discussion while really I was leaving my wife there with the Midwestern culture experts and going back to our room to watch Italian programming on a thirteen-inch television with a coat-hanger antenna. At one time, our room had been the rabbit hutch. Probably I am interpreting the specific wording in my own way, but the word *rabbit* was definitely employed. The rabbit hutch, like its chimney, was essentially open-air, and if you opened a window in the midsummer heat, you found there were no screens on the windows. We were told, when we asked, that there were screens— *Yes! We will fetch them, yes!*—but no screens materialized, and here in the land of only recently eradicated malaria, the local mosquitoes descended on us with a force such as I have rarely encountered. Every night at dusk there was a swarm around my head, and the swarm stayed until morning unless I pulled the sheets over me entirely. Eventually I needed to come up for air. My upper lip swelled from the volume of clotting agent injected into it by the mosquito hordes, and I had to give one or two classes looking like a boxer fresh from some KO.

In the afternoons, we would go out to see things in the area around Puglia, like a chapel that was filled with the bones of martyrs, or some thatched cottages called *trulli* that looked like the backdrop for an elvish fantasy spectacular. We went to the tip of the boot heel of Italia, Leuca, to see the Adriatic and the Mediterranean meet, and there were a lot of attractive young Italians there eating gelato. We were not them. One day we were on our way to see some mosaic somewhere—Otranto, I think—and my wife became sick from the heat and had to sit down or have some food, and I began to feel in that moment that my obligation to teach, and my vanishing from dinner to watch Italian television on my own, and her inability to keep up on the long marches of tourism were disparate examples of the pain that is vacation.

One night, toward the end of our stay, we noticed that the birds in the birdcage in the center of the farm had disappeared since that morning. What had looked so lovely and symbolic in the morning, a mating pair of some lovely species, destined to replenish their numbers in the fullness of theological time, was now symbolic only of loss, a few feathers, some bird shit, and kernels of cracked corn. My wife realized at once what we should have realized all along, namely, that we had been eating the birds. Every day a different bird, and it had seemed so picturesque, so fecund, and really it was just about the myriad ways you could kill those animals. Had the others known what we were too naive to know? That night at dinner, in broken Italian, we asked the Ernest Borgnine proprietor to tell us what had happened to the pair of grouse or pheasants or turkeys or chickens that had been in the cage that morning, and he looked up at the ceiling and without a trace of a smile said, *They have gone to their Heavenly Father.* Everyone had a good laugh.

This was the moment that I felt my marriage beginning to give out. It seems preposterous to say so, because we were only some few years into it and it would be years more before there was ever a discussion of our separating, and this was a trip, despite some routine tribulations, that we later thought back on with some amusement. But what is that little shearing away that takes place that somehow you can't repair? How does that happen, when it happens against your will? When there are many other such moments that you willingly tolerate or let go of without incident? There are rows, shouting matches, secreted away or even in public that seem so much worse but that are followed by sweet reunion, and why is this the moment that later appears to be when things started to go wrong? Here we were, laughing on a beach on the Adriatic, watching the Italian families with their not terribly flattering bathing suits playing in the grainy uncomfortable sand, and gazing out together on the still Adriatic, with its effluvial tide of Albanians on their fragments of boats rowing across and landing in some ditch in the middle of an olive grove and sleeping on a mattress in that ditch, all so they could come to the old, grizzled, implacable Europe.

Back then I could still remember a first kiss in some hotel in Detroit, and a time when she still wanted to whisper something in my ear and would set a cup of tea in front of me in the morning. It would just appear. To any outside observer all was fine, and in Puglia there was a dish of olives the day before, and there would be a dish of olives again that night containing olives as good as any I had ever tasted, and by first kiss I mean the kind of rhetorical kiss that says the future is of milk and honey. I could still have remembered it there, and maybe the Italian families could still remember such things too, could remember when they had been young and riding around on motorbikes, not bent out of shape with children and responsibilities, but simply young and untroubled and beautiful and eating gelato, three or four of them beautiful and hanging off a motorbike careening down a one-way street in the dark with no headlights, no helmets, going forty-five miles an hour and barely missing some Fiat racing around a curve, laughing, the dumb luck of it all, the dumb luck of the Mediterranean sun, the perfect light of Renaissance painting; maybe the Italians remembered all of that, and on the days when they needed to, they thought back on it. Why was this the moment that I gave up? The predictable failure of lovers over time was at least something you could warm yourself with on a long winter night. Like the mixed blessing of vacation. ★★ *(Posted 3/2/2014)*

Hampton Inn and Suites, 33 West Illinois Street, Chicago, Illinois, March 21–22, 1996

I had heard about her from a friend in New York. My friend said I should meet his friend in Chicago. It was actually Detroit, in all honesty, but as these reviews are appearing in a public forum, I'm going to say it was Chicago, and I have made up a hotel and an address, and you will simply have to believe me that this hotel is exactly like the hotel in question, and thus my rating is accurate, even if it is accurate only by analogy.

It was the early days of this life that is now increasingly common, by which I mean the online life, the life where I ply my trade as a top-rated hotel reviewer. I was already having a number of affairs with people I didn't know in the real world, but only in the so-called chat rooms of online life, those early features that have now given way to random mutual masturbation in video with Muscovites, and so for the early part of our association, which lasted about a week, we spoke mainly in this online way, and she had no face, so far as I knew, and could easily have been a housewife from Kansas with IBS and multiple-personality disorder. I didn't care so much about her real identity; the simulation of an identity was adequate enough for the time being. For a few days we did that dance where your identity is a collision of citations—books, recordings, musicals, films—and then a number of snapshots that you re-create in some fit of idealized self, and she passed all the tests, meaning that she adhered very faithfully to a fantasy idea of a woman with whom I might be involved, if in fact I was ever going to be involved with another woman rather than just some humiliating magazines or online avatars.

I had no particular reason to believe that she existed. Nevertheless, it occurred to me, and here I was way ahead of the curve in the digital world, that maybe I ought to meet her, just to avoid wasting weeks more of time, several hours a night, talking to her in chat rooms and wondering if she was on a respirator or had only one limb. We discussed this and, incredibly, were in perfect agreement about how to proceed, though perhaps less incredibly when one recalls that in the early frothy period of talking to someone who doesn't have a body, who is a brain in a vat, you agree about everything. In my mind she was tall, thin, blue-eyed, and brunette, with her nose just slightly off-center and perhaps a gap between her front teeth, and she liked to wear denim with a few rips in it, but not too many, and she wore cheap sneakers and liked thrift-store clothes, especially bowling shirts. It would be useful, I felt, to compare this imagined person with the real person, who happened to live in Chicago. I had been in Chicago for business once or twice, because I had been most everywhere. Usually I stayed in the Loop, not seeing much of the city besides, and I was looking forward to seeing some of the city in a more relaxed way. I believe my father, from whom I was estranged, as I might have mentioned, also lived in Chicago at one time. Though I had no interest in chasing down the facts of my father's life, his having lived there did leave an afterglow on the city for me. And who knew—perhaps the father who had fled was just a few blocks over from John Wayne Gacy's house. Maybe my father too had learned how to contact women online, pretending to be a luxury car dealer with a double-breasted suit and a power tie who was looking for someone who enjoyed hiking and single-malt Scotch whisky.

I flew out on American Airlines and met her just beyond security, which was a lot different in those bygone days, no shoe bomber yet, liquids permitted. I was a young man in my thirties who still believed that the world was ahead of him, striding through the airport as though the striding were important, and I was meeting the short brown-eyed blonde with the bangs on the far side of security. And there she was—greeting me with her barrage of sunny verbiage that didn't seem to slow down for any purpose: *Hey how was your flight okay did you sit on the aisle or the window I always like to sit on the aisle well actually I don't know which I like because I don't fly that much but if I did fly I would like the aisle because if you think about it the aisle causes the least interruption in your flight and what did you read did you read the flight magazine do you like to look at the airport layout in the flight magazines do you ever do the crosswords in the back I have thought of some things for us to see in Chicago if you haven't thought of anything to see I mean it's great if you have thought of some things to see but if you haven't thought of any things to see you probably didn't know that Chicago is one of America's greatest cities for architecture and it's that way because of the fire you know about the fire right well the fire wasn't really set by a cow just in case you think it was set by a cow that's just a story they tell anyway so a lot of buildings needed to get rebuilt quickly after the fire and I can show you some of the buildings and tell you why they're important because actually I work for one of the wealthiest families in Chicago it's a real estate company and I'm the office manager for this family and so I know a lot about Chicago real estate I have seen it up close and did you know that river floods a lot and there are problems with the basements of a lot of these buildings because of the flooding.*

On it would go until something physically stopped it, like we had to get into a taxi, which I was paying for, and find a restaurant to eat in, and we ate in a Thai restaurant, and she had some story about how she and her friends always ate in this particular Thai restaurant because it had a cheap Thai night, and she kept getting up, with a kind of joyful sigh, to go call her best friend on the pay phone, to inform her friend that she had not yet been cut up into pieces and shoved into a freezer. I have no idea what kind of impression I made, but I suspect I did not make much of a good impression. I don't know that I have ever made a good impression.

I had booked one night at the hotel (she picked it, by the way), because if things went badly I'd be gone in a day, and if things went well, I could always come back. We went back to the hotel to take our clothes off immediately, as though this were our only purpose, and I recollect that this was about loneliness, as far as I was concerned. The thing you did to alleviate the loneliness was to take off your clothes and touch someone, even if you didn't really know the person well. I could just as easily have asked her to let me lie down on top of her fully clothed on a couch in the lobby of the Hampton Inn and Suites, but I didn't know that then. I thought I was supposed to take off my clothes, and I wanted her to take off her clothes, and somehow this seemed a foregone conclusion, perhaps because each of us had started with no face and no body, as a condition of modern life, and now we were here and we wanted to celebrate the fact that we were not hideous, not entirely, and we were in the flesh.

It was at this point, I believe, that she indicated it was that time of the month. (Yes, for those who would read the back catalog, see my review of the Hotel Equinox of Manchester, Vermont. Never the romance without the bloodshed!) Again, I want it to be on the record that I could provide a sturdy facsimile of love under any circumstances. We did what men and women do. Later, we went down to the lobby, while some poor underpaid room-service technician had the job of removing the evidence. I must conclude that the maid service was adequate, as the police were not contacted, and we went back in the room and did the whole thing over.

You might imagine that this would be a predictor, in the next decade and a half (more or less), of some gymnastic approach to the conjugal act, a prognostic of a mutual commitment to the arts of physical pleasure, even if the rest of the relationship fell to pieces around our heads. But no! We quickly reverted to some quiet desperation in the years following, wishing even as we engaged in our rote connubial relations that the state of desire could be hours long again, despairing about the loss of it, feeling at first a numbness and then even irritation, each for the other, in some kind of hopeless yen to allow ourselves to give up on the relationship, a longing that for some reason could not quite be effected, so that we experienced at once both devotion and betrayal, love and contempt, each motive at the same time, watching the years tick by. Who is to blame for all of that? Can we somehow blame the Hampton Inn and Suites? I stayed the night, alone, and sent my future wife back to the apartment she was living in without her former boyfriend, who had uncouth tendencies and against whom she had filed a restraining order. I was the most decent, most reasonable person she had gone out with in at least a year, the kind of guy who in high school was again and again and again some girl's *pal*, and perhaps even my wife wanted me only as a pal.

Perhaps now I should tell you, as I have not told you in any other review that I have written here on RateYourLodging.com, that I cannot sleep without a pillow over my face, and thus it would be really easy to asphyxiate me, and perhaps my future wife, when I had fallen into narcolepsy after the first bloody round of lovemaking, might very well have executed me if she wanted to steer her fate away from a decade and a half of grief and progressive estrangement among both parties; instead, there I was that night, by myself, with a pillow over my face, probably getting insufficient amounts of oxygen and thus risking stroke, and I was thinking about how great the whole thing was, how great it was going to be, it was all going to be great, the fluorescent bulbs of the Loop twinkling below, the trains going around on the Loop like some monstrously scaled replication of a Lionel train set, the Chicago Bulls in the middle of a great season, it was all going to be great, because I had just had sex twice with a woman who was not in fact a Kansas housewife with IBS and multiple-personality disorder, and I had flown out to Chicago for this very purpose, which was a sign that I had grown into the completion of adulthood and masculinity, and I was enough moved by my hotel experience that I got up and located a piece of stationery in the desk next to the Gideon and with just the light from the window I scrawled out a thank-you note for the maid, and I set it on the desk and laid a crisp twenty beside it. It was all going to be so great. ★★★★ *(Posted 3/8/2014)*

The Capri Whitestone, 555 Hutchinson River Parkway North, Bronx, New York, March 7–22, 2014

What is it we really want from hotel life? We want the closest thing we can get to home. We want a reminder that home exists—that place you can come back to after a long inadvisable journey where they are in theory happy to see you. A place where the pillow awaits the impression of your head. A place where when you step in out of the rain, you breathe a sigh of relief. A place where everything broken was broken by you or by people you care about. A place where you could close your eyes and, more or less, make your way around just fine. A place at the end of a road you know well. A place where, should you suddenly become afflicted with a total absence of memory, it is reasonable to suppose that you would be returned.

Home, the place your enemies would wish to avoid. Home, the place your former lovers are troubled by. Home, where you can sit at the quiet table in the morning. Home, the place you sometimes hate that you also love the second you leave it. Home, any address that causes you to tear up. Home, near the metal box that has your surname on it. Home, where almost all the postcards you have ever received have been delivered. Home, where the government of your nation believes you live. Home, where your mother or your father brought you the second you no longer lived in a hospital. Home, where you first sang whatever it is you first sang. What *welcome* means, this you first learned at home, along with the word *home*. Home is where your bedroom was in the past and is now, and home is where you sleep more days than you sleep anywhere else, because if it were otherwise, you would renegotiate the application of the word *home*. Home is where there is almost always a beverage that you like. Home is where, if you wait long enough, it is likely that you will be fed a dessert even if it is not the best thing for you to eat. Home is where you are able to watch your favorite programs. Home is where people will try to find you when they need to find you. Home is the address you will sneak out of to kiss the first person you ever kiss who is not a member of your family, and it is the place to which you will return afterward, knowing about that kiss. Home is where you will first learn about disappointment, and it is where you will learn that it is okay to feel disappointed. Home is the place that is almost always indicated with a final major chord. Home, when you are older, is where you will watch your children grow, and, in fact, no other way of describing home is as valuable and meaningful as this, and when you are near death, the impossible sweetness of life will adhere first and foremost to the home where you watched your child or your children grow, or where you watched other neighborhood children grow, watched them rise up from the carpet and stab at something with their little paws before attempting to stick it into their mouths. This will be your home. Home may also be the place where they have called you an asshole more than any other place. Home is where you will paint your masterpiece. Home is what you will describe in your masterpiece; either home or the leaving of home. If you say you have no home on earth, then what you mean is that there was trouble at your home. Home is where you go right before dark. Home is where you go when you are recovered. When work becomes impossible, you will long for home. It is possible that in your life you have had multiple homes, a sequence of homes, and that each of these has required a transition. For example, when you were in a car that carried you from a house where both of your parents had lived together to a house where only one of your parents lived, even during that car ride, there was still an idea of home.

That catch in your throat that is the feeling that you will never be known, never be esteemed? That feeling evaporates in the presence of home fires, and while no substitute is adequate, there is the sense in the finest hotels that you are not far from home. When you embark on your journey, you set aside this notion of home, as if launching onto a whitecapped sea, certain that you are sturdy enough to let go of home, to relinquish the familiar, but it is only because you know that you can return home again, and it is the job of the hotel, the inn, the motel, the furnished room, to suggest the possibility of home or serve as a way station for home, preparing you for that return, lightening the load as long as you must be away.

This is the great romance of life, the losing of home temporarily as when, upon that same storm-tossed sea, you lost the horizon line. The hotel helps you to see the horizon, even if there is no land to be witnessed there.

Or so it has been in the recent, modern centuries of human history, and so it would continue to be if it were not for one tiny nettlesome bit of insect life that has emerged from up out of the eons of the past like a scourge to torpedo the serenity of our home lives, and that nettlesome life-form, as you must recognize by now, is the *bedbug*. Where did the bedbug come from? It came from somewhere in the evolutionary past, the dark ages, and it came to disturb your sleep, so that you would never sleep again, and while resting comfortably, you would wake to a stabbing pain on the surface of some extremity; somewhere the blood is pooling in such a way that the bedbug can come at you for warmth, creature comfort, and a full belly. It was gone, this species, but now it has returned, and it has descended on the cities, almost all places where there are hotels in abundance, and everyone you know, whether virtuous or sinful and carefree, is a potential vector of the dreaded bedbug.

Do you know any musicians? Do you know musicians from Francophone Canada who live in a sort of a commune and practice community ownership of their possessions and who do not wash their hair as often as they might? These musicians are almost certain to be harboring bedbugs, especially after a year of touring and sleeping on various people's floors. Do not let them into your house. There are bedbugs in their guitar cases or their duffel bags. Every cinema that you visit carries with it the possibility of bedbugs, especially if it is not newly renovated, as in the old chain theaters that attract a downmarket clientele. You are better off not bringing any personal possessions, such as knapsacks or briefcases,

into this movie theater. And then there are the hotels. It is widely
known that even some of the best hotels in the nation have had
outbreaks of these critters, and probably they bomb entire floors
or strip them down to the studs before re-releasing the rooms onto
the market. How do you know if they have eliminated the problem
or not? I have stayed in some fine hotels in my day, but I was in
no way certain in any of them that I would be unmolested by the
bedbug.

At one time, the bedbug was a class marker. It separated the
wannabes from the dynasts. Power is not afraid of powerful insec-
ticides. But these things no longer separate us, for we are all fallen
into the abyss of bedbug-related chaos. Some guy from Mali gets
a visa because he is being tortured for his religious beliefs, and
brings the hemorrhagic virus with him on the flight from London. Another guy comes from Pattaya with the antibiotic-resistant
strain of gonorrhea. It's all one world now, the bedbugs cry out,
and they gather up resolve in the neighborhoods of addicts, where
people have stopped washing or cleaning, and these addicts take
them to the motels where they are putting up for a day or two to
get their heads together before going home to tell their husbands
or wives that they have spent it all.

The bedbugs await these administrations of sorrow, and then
they move on to the truckers, the truckers slumbering off a
seventy-two-hour shift, so wasted and dead inside that they
wouldn't know if the bedbugs took off a six-inch patch of them, and
the truckers in turn take them from one state to the next, or else the
truckers pass them on to the hookers, because what trucker does
not, at some point in his dismal haul, squint out into the parking
lot and see in dim light the woman who does not look all that bad.
The trucker comes from where we are most impoverished, and he
brings the bedbugs, and when the bedbugs arrive in the city, they

find an unimaginably colorful banquet laid out before them, a feast of human tissue, because where one human is neat and clean and somewhat cautious about such things, only fifty feet away lives a deranged and toothless hoarder of decayed snacks and tchotchkes whose apartment features a bounty of rats and cockroaches and un-read copies of *USA Today*. So many places for the bedbugs to get comfortable, and when they are comfortable and have a base of operations, they move out to colonize.

What does this mean for the hotel guest? What does the bed-bug mean for the likes of you and me as we check into another hotel? You know me, you know my wish to tell the truth, whether it is good for the operators of the hotels or good for their guests. I bring you the facts, no matter how controversial. I came to the Capri Whitestone, with its view of the Whitestone Bridge toll plaza, because I had booked the room online and there was a bargain price, and then I got here and realized there was no bathroom in my room, that it was down the hall, and that my bathroom, down the hall, was being used by itinerant preach-ers and opium addicts and appliance sales executives. And so I determined that I would not use the bathroom in the hallway, because whatever had been in that bathroom was at least partly rotted out, gangrenous; there was the overpowering reverberation of death in that bathroom, and the attendant sense of grief in the Capri Whitestone led me away from the bathroom and down the hall back to my room.

Since I had no desire to get up in the middle of the night and head down the hall, I instead took to using the sink in my bed-room, easier said than done. (I'm not proud of this, understand, and I don't like admitting it in my column, though I think the Capri Whitestone should feel worse about this than I do.) I had to bring the rickety desk chair, really just a folding aluminum thing such as you could get at any office-supply store, over to the sink and stand on the chair, and then I had to find an angle that would permit a minimum of splashing. Afterward I hung my overnight bag in just the way you would tree your food if you were out in the forest, living off the land. My sleep at the Capri Whitestone was an unquiet sleep, and even the decades-old television on the shelf could not help me, with its meager array of programs about bachelors and bachelorettes; the remote had never seemed so well named. The whole first night was spent trying not to think about the most adaptable of pests, the bedbug.

In this edition of clinically diagnosed insomnia, I was thinking instead about seeing my kid the next day and about the fact that recently I have been seeing her alone, unaccompanied by K., who is back in Yonkers, refusing me admittance until the relapse that occurred after the Florida trip has passed. Look, some people think that relapse of the variety I am describing here happens because the cares of the world come elbowing in, and that in the double bind of these cares, there is no choice but to give in. If you had my life, you would do it too, etc. But I am here to say that sometimes it is when things go well that we get in a gypsy cab, drive to a honky-tonk dive on the Jersey shore, sleep under a pier in our clothes, drink rye whiskey for several days running, solicit the professional women in the industrial park, vomit on ourselves, sing unwanted classic-rock tunes in public places, whisper contemptuously to ourselves, and then take the train back to the city, sitting in the rearmost car so that no one will be forced to reckon with us, wondering how to spin the narrative of our episodic disappearance. Sometimes it's the good stuff that causes this, sometimes it's love and a week of Indian summer, it's the bounty of life, or it's so without cause as to be a perfect example of what goes by the fell name *human nature.*

So I take the child to the movies or to a restaurant or to other such public places, but not back to my hotel room here at the Capri Whitestone—from which I am writing this review—for reasons that will be obvious to anyone who has read the lines above. Under the circumstances, I have to admire the rock-bottom price of the Capri Whitestone, and yet my stay here has ensured that the child and I have no home to go back to, not really, and this has been the hardest thing of all, the inability to deploy that semantic warhorse *home* with reliable consistency. I could live at a great number of motels of the tristate area, like the Rodeway Bronx or the West Shore Staten Island, but I have landed here because the Capri has easy access to major thoroughfares of the region, such as the Bruckner Expressway, the Van Wyck Expressway, I-95, the Hutchinson River Parkway, the Pelham Parkway, the Cross Bronx Expressway, the Major Deegan Expressway, the Sprain Brook Parkway, the Saw Mill River Parkway, and the Cross County Parkway, and this proximity seems enough, while waiting for the grip of relapse to unclench.

I can feel, in the sometimes stilted conversation between myself and the child, the future when we will not talk as well or as easily as we usually do now, when she will ask questions about why I have lived the way I have lived, and I won't be able to answer, except to say that I have lived the way I knew how to live, *hic et nunc.* I am a father who wanted at all costs to keep his daughter away from bedbugs. And that is something. Her mother has the pies to bake and the blankets to tuck around her, that song of femininity that no father can give, and what have I but some meager store of words that have fogged up the windows of progress and distracted a few people over the years? They are the same words that I have always used, and now they are careworn. Okay, bachelorettes. ★ *(Posted 3/22/2014)*

The Guest of Honor, 131 Cricket Hill Road, Lakeville, Connecticut, February 6–7, 2010

KoWojahk283 and others have accused me of failing to review bed-and-breakfasts on RateYourLodging.com, and I must admit that this charge, as distinct from many other charges I have detailed elsewhere, is in fact true. I have not reviewed any bed-and-breakfasts. And the reason is simple: because I hate bed-and-breakfast inns. What's the problem with B&Bs, as they are often called among the types of people who prefer these inns? First, there is the issue of throw-pillow abuse. It is as if the throw pillow were a sign of affluence. There must be some kind of bed-and-breakfast trade association where the various owners get together and compete on how many throw pillows they have in their various rooms. The second problem, as is widely known, is the scented product called potpourri. Why is it that potpourri is so uniformly understood as the solution to the olfactory problem of the B&B? Potpourri is meant to cleanse the air of any human residue and to render neutral even the most foul-smelling traveler so that he seems to hail from a knickknack shop in Sedona, Arizona. That everyone has agreed that this one particular smell—of orange, sandalwood, lavender, cinnamon, and a hint of cocoa—is the idealized scent of human exchange is bizarre. There's a desperation to the brutal efficiency of the potpourri solution.

The third, and biggest, problem of the B&B, however, is the breakfast itself. In a way, I'm being facetious here, because everyone will admit that the food at these breakfasts—*The honey comes from our own apiary!*—is some of the best food you are ever liable to eat. It's not that the food is bad. I could probably put away forty-five hundred calories at one of these breakfasts and go back for more. The issue with the breakfasts is the human conversation. I would subdivide this conversation into two separate categories. The first of these categories includes the conversation you must have with the innkeeper herself. The innkeeper, though she is pleasant, is worried that you are a barely concealed sociopath, and when she allows you into her house, she makes especially sure to lock the doors that lead to her private residence. She has the local authorities on speed dial and is on a first-name basis with these local authorities, and all her conversation, no matter how simplistic or unsophisticated, can be understood as exploratory, in which she is attempting to make a quick but reliable mental-health determination. So when the innkeeper says, *Such a shame about the rain!*, you can bet that she doesn't really mind the precipitation, especially if she has already taken an impression of your Visa card, but is instead trying to judge how the precipitation might affect your own mien. And when she asks a couple of leading questions about your reasons for being in the area, she breathes an almost palpable sigh of relief when she realizes that you are touring. The prattle of the innkeeper, then, while a colossal waste of your time, is not to be understood as anything but legitimate research. The same cannot be said for conversation track two, conversation with other persons staying at the bed-and-breakfast establishment. It is of the utmost importance that you establish, with these other persons, a reputation for ill humor and an absolute inability to be lucid before a certain hour. You can allude to a chronic dependence on caffeinated hot beverages. Sometimes it is useful to produce a pill jar containing medication. Whatever the technique, it is essential that you do not begin conversation with the other couple, however mild-mannered they appear, lest you should begin to discuss other bed-and-breakfasts (almost as if the bed-and-breakfast is capable only of creating an environment in which one must endlessly lobby on behalf of the bed-and-breakfast as institution), or fastest routes from Boston to the Maine coast, or prettiest churches in the neighborhood, or most spectacular weekends spent leaf-peeping. Upon making conversation, it is further possible that you will have to exchange e-mail addresses with the couple or that they will invite you to dinner that night at a farm-to-table restaurant in the vicinity. This is why abysmal hotels in the Midwest where the only thing you can have for breakfast is Wheaties are somehow superior to the B&B experience, because at least there you don't have to explain.

To summarize, these are the three main problems of bed-and-breakfast establishments: throw pillows, potpourri, and breakfast conversation, and the fourth problem is gazebos. And the fifth problem is water features. And the sixth problem is themed rooms, and the seventh problem is provenance (who owned the inn before and who owned the inn before that, and who owned it before that, and what year the bed-and-breakfast was built, and how old the timber is in the main hall), and the eighth problem is pride of ownership, because why can't it just be a place you stay, why does it always have to be an ideological crusade? And the ninth problem is excessive amounts of regional advice. And the tenth problem is the absence of telephones. Even if you aren't going to use the telephone, you want to know that the telephone is there. And the eleventh problem is price. There is no bed-and-breakfast that you can see from the interstate that says $39.95 in a neon sign above it, and although you can really sleep peacefully in the bed-and-breakfast if you are the sort of person who can be comfortable in the presence of a superabundance of pillows, that rush of uncertainty and danger that you get from the motel by the interstate is absent.

Well, given the feelings described above, you are probably wondering why I would go to a bed-and-breakfast after all this. And to speak to this question I have to speak of the way in which I met K. In the more than two years that I have been working as an online reviewer of hotels, I have never told you this very pertinent detail about my personal life, and that is the way in which I met K., the love of my life (even though it appears, at the time of this writing, that I am still in a hotel by myself, trying to avoid using the bathroom down the hall, which is exactly how I described it in my review of yesterday). It happens that about the time my ex-wife and I signed the relevant documents related to our parting, I went to a local ashram, which I had learned about from a flyer on the bulletin board at a local health-food provider, whose aisles I was wandering aimlessly because I had nowhere else to go. There in the foyer, among the advertisements for home-birth classes and guitar lessons and clutter clearing, I saw a flyer for open classes in meditation and thought-cleansing. I noticed immediately that whoever had written the copy for this advertisement of meditation and thought-cleansing did not have a real grasp on the kinds of marketing language that would drive a person into a class on meditation and thought-cleansing, and so I resolved that I would offer my services at the ashram in the hopes that I might serve in some kind of official function.

I marked down the address, and then on the day of the meditation and thought-cleansing session, I took a bus over to the neighborhood in question. (I'm leaving out the precise address of the ashram, because I would prefer that the kindness of the ashram remain a kindness unknown to the likes of TigerBooty! or KoWojahk283 or WakeAndBake.) I had no intention of meditating and did not believe my thoughts were in any need of cleansing. My idea was to petition the monk or monks about the advertisement, but I turned up at the ashram a little bit late, and because I was late, I had no choice but to sit in on the class. There was a flurry of activity around me, as some people with shaved heads indicated where the seating pads were and helped me to find a place. The sensei, or howsoever he was called, was giving his little talk, and it was about the course of thought, which, in the view of the sensei, was about flailing in the dark, lost, and the goal was not to think at all but to create some free-floating stasis in which one's thoughts were like billboards and you just drove on past them and didn't order the product. This seemed like a good plan, and quaint, as I'd heard many people saying things like this thirty years ago, but the plan was also difficult for me because of the pitch I was going to make about how the advertisements they were using for the ashram could be improved.

I had so many good marketing ideas, but then in the middle of the sensei's lecture I must have begun listening to him. We were supposed to have our eyes closed, but I couldn't help but notice that there was a woman next to me, with dark hair and modern racial chemistry, who was wearing some rather fetching yoga pants and a black T-shirt and who seemed to be in deepest concentration. Apparently, cleansing my thoughts was making me forget my mercantile purpose, and instead I was thinking about the woman, but even in this area I was prey to the oceanic intonements of the sensei, his half-Japanese muttering, because somewhere in the middle of the hour, which seemed more like seven or eight hours, I began either to drift off or to feel some sense of well-being, which I guess implies an absence of worry about money, and perhaps there were fifteen minutes or so of thinking about only the woman, and then maybe there was a period, an elevated echelon, where I felt the stirrings of something that, to my horror, corresponded with what was being described by the sensei, that is, the beginnings of contentment.

It would be reasonable to ask whether these were actually cleansing thoughts or something closer to mind control, but given that there was time left on the clock for that day's class, I could not but give in, and off I went, and I would say, as readers of the Rate Your Lodging site might be aware, that I have trouble getting my thoughts to *decelerate*. Does anyone else have trouble with that kind of thing? It was sort of a miracle for me to find that the sensei and his voice had now receded beyond the waves of meditative space, and I was finding that actually the quiet was agreeable, and even the slight knee pain was no real nuisance, and that it was as though I were the skiff, and the cares of my life had been left behind in a cooler on a dock, and now I was dropping the lines and setting out onto the pond. The pond's shores withdrew as I rowed, and now I was in and of the current, and the current was strong, I no longer needed to row at all, and the pond had become a lake, and above the lake, dusk fell into its painterly tonalities.

And this was how I learned that I was of the ocean. I was the clock coming to a stop, I was the strings that don't get played but just vibrate sympathetically, I was the nest awaiting its fledglings, I was the coming of night, I was the bicycle cresting the hill, I was the music box, I was the windmill turning with no one around to watch, I was the tree in the forest, I was the choir whose individual voices could no longer be distinguished, I was the clouds after the storm, I was the table awaiting its cornucopia, I was the bed awaiting its sleeper, I was the book passed from hand to hand, I was the reverberations of the muezzin having called the city to prayer, I was the hand waiting to be held, I was the ropes for the climb, I was the hammock out back, I was the song of the songbird, I was the old sand washed to the top of the new in the sequence of waves, I was the teardrop in the moment of being wiped away, I was the aerodynamics of the bumblebee, I was the stairs up to the proscenium, I was the cage door swinging open, I was part of the other people in the ashram, I was starting to feel that I *was* the other people in the room, though I was the unlikeliest person in the room to have had this beginner's luck in the meditation and cleansing thoughts, and I didn't have time to think about that, I could see the woman in black and feel something coming from her toward me, as if we were one together, though at the moment, I also felt this way about any number of other people in the room, like the guy with the gray comb-over and the lavender headband. I felt one with him and his callused feet, and with the anorexic woman in the corner wearing sunglasses, with her gallon-size jug of water; I was one with all of them.

Gently the sensei began to call us forth, and although I would like to claim it was an impossibility that I had been asleep, it was not an impossibility, and the calling forth was an eruption of life and its cares into the room, which didn't look like an ashram but like somebody's apartment with a few cushions strewn about. Soon people were gathering up their stuff, and others were approaching the sensei, if that's who he was, and bowing, and so I guessed that I needed to go over and bow to him too, so I went over, and as I went over I realized that now I was standing in the company of the woman, the woman I had been thinking of, and I listened as she thanked the sensei and bowed, and then he was turning to me and he was saying that he hadn't seen me there before, and I said, *Yes, that's true, it's my first time,* and he asked what had brought me there, and I told him that I had actually seen the flyer in the store of the local health-food purveyor, and he said, *Oh, my brother, you have no idea how good those flyers are! Priceless advertising, really. And they don't require much effort!* As you can imagine, this remark kind of ruined my pitch, which I had been composing with my superior rhetorical skills in the days since I saw the flyer. I was so nonplussed by his observations that I couldn't think what to say, and so I smiled like one of the happy converted.

Kay, the sensei said, *how is that period of bereavement coming now, are you feeling better, are you able to get out and do things a bit?* And K. said something in reply, which I did not catch, because I heard, in this remark by the sensei, the bereavement that this woman faced, and I knew at once that I could be part of the solution. I could be the person who helped her into the next phase of her life, and all I had to do was convince her of this in the next few crucial minutes. The way I saw it, I needed, as soon as her exchange with the sensei was done, to find myself a step behind her as she made her way to the cubbies by the entrance, where I would engage her in light conversation, afterward trying to ascertain her next destination and then, if possible, accompany her. Because, after all, we were one. One mind, one self.

The sensei said something about looking forward to seeing her again, and of course I wondered whether he had put his filthy Eastern-inflected paws on K., but there was no time for that, because now she was heading for her personal effects, and I, in my khaki trousers and worn oxford-cloth shirt, was right behind. A few others lingered by the doorway talking about this and that, some vegan treat they were preparing that night. I said to K., *Would you like to go for a quick cup of coffee? I consider myself a sympathetic listener in the area of bereavement counseling. Indeed, I am bereaved myself.* And she said: *You don't even know what my bereavement is about.* And she fixed on me a look at once skeptical and amused. I was already gathering up my things, a knapsack and sweater, and we were moving toward the door, but then I was stopped by one of the employees, a minion, and was asked if I had perhaps forgotten something. Now the minion was telling me how much the suggested donation was for me to sit and have my thoughts cleansed, and I did not want to appear insolvent in front of K., so I quickly pulled out a few crisp bills and presented them, after which the minion asked if I wanted to fill out a questionnaire about my first time at the ashram, and I looked at him and then looked at K., radiant, unearthly, and then we were out the door.

There's not a chance in the world you're going to believe what happened next, which is to say the unlikely antecedent of this particular review, so I have no choice, in the end, but to try to use a few words to describe my thinking at the time. I don't imagine that anyone believes love was possible after a mere hour spent sitting in the ashram when most of the meditation time our eyes were closed, but why, then, did K. say the thing she said to me only minutes after we had collected our Americanos and arranged ourselves by the window in a nearby café? You see, the truth is that all conversion experiences are really experiences of love. What I have said I have said, in the matter of the hotels of North America, and I can say now, with confidence, that most of the hotels in North America are not very good hotels, at least not the ones in my price range, and they are places where a long-ago idea of entrepreneurship and customer service has gone to perish. Many hotels and motels of North America are like the Capri Whitestone, and after a point, there is no further purpose in reviewing the hotels of North America, especially if your employer, the Rate Your Lodging website, is going to be absorbed into a larger conglomerate, at which time all freelance positions, and indeed any of the scrappy, upstart energy of the formerly shaggy and handmade operation, will be subject to intervention by corporate apologists and by their accountants and fembot publicists. But the main reason to leave off reviewing is because now I have given an account of love. What else is there to say? So we were sitting on the stools at the front of a café, talking about this and that, when K. said to me, *Why don't we drive north and check into a bed-and-breakfast?* ★ ★ ★ ★ *(Posted 3/8/2014)*

Afterword

by Rick Moody

It was mid-2014, about the time the Rate Your Lodging website was absorbed into the Dynasty Inc. family of publications, that I was approached by one of the former staff editors about writing an afterword to the collected writings of Reginald Edward Morse. Morse, whose manuscript I was then given, was a reviewer who had inspired a healthy readership among the devotees of Rate Your Lodging and sometimes even beyond. There seemed no reason at all to agree to write this afterword. The fee was insubstantial, the deadline was nigh, and I am not the sort of person who goes online to read reviews. Reginald Morse, whoever he was—and I will speculate on this below—was not a William Faulkner, or even a Molly Ivins or a Mitch Albom. He was a guy practicing a homely craft. There are lots and lots of these people out there, cranking out posts about books, movies, recordings, doctors, professors, accountants, appliances, plumbers, hotels. They believe in what they do. I think it's admirable. But that didn't mean I needed to help out.

I had decided to reject the offer, therefore, despite the honor of the request, until the day on which I had lunch with a freelance editor retained by RateYourLodging.com to assemble this book project you hold in your hands. This is when I became aware of what I would call the mystery of Reginald Morse. Michelle

Perry, the editor in question, explained to me over the course of lunch that Morse seemed to have vanished not long after posting a final review in March of 2014. He had posted monthly, or twice monthly, beginning in 2012 and continued for more than two years, reviews that from the outset were often ambitious in length and scope, with scant attention paid, in some cases, to the actual hotels being reviewed, in order for him to write about identity, intimacy, loneliness, and love. Nothing in his demeanor, in his excesses of verbiage, indicated that he had any reason to put down his pen. And yet on the first Friday in April 2014, there was suddenly a silence, and thereafter Morse failed to communicate with R. Jahna, his in-house contact, nor did he ever turn in further reviews. That was the last that the Rate Your Lodging website ever heard from Reginald Morse. At least, as of this writing.

It is true, isn't it, that the inner mechanics of even our closest acquaintances are a mystery to us? It is true that our suppositions about character can be reversed in a moment. There are large parts of all of us that lie hidden, both unmapped and unpredictable. Apparently, Reginald Morse, if that's even his name, had more hidden than most.

For example: Michelle Perry, while assembling these pages, used payroll data to track the author to an address on the Upper West Side of New York City, an apartment never once alluded to in Morse's prose output. Perry, in fact, taxied up to Morse's presumptive building and waited around until a superintendent made himself obvious, at which point she ventured a few inoffensive queries designed to bulk out the biography of the writer of this collection. Did the superintendent perhaps know a man called Reginald Morse? Had the superintendent seen a tall middle-aged balding man, a little bit heavyset, living on the fifth floor (per the payroll stubs, he lived in 5C)? With, perhaps, a female companion?

The super, according to Perry, pointed out that almost every floor in the building had its share of balding heavyset men, though he did admit that he knew of at least one or two people on the fifth floor who might have fitted the description: affable, talkative, unemployed. On the basis of this scanty information, Michelle Perry waited around for a couple of hours, marking up this manuscript with a red pencil in the process, and did the same on a couple of subsequent days, without ever catching a glimpse of Morse himself. Indeed, it turned out in a few weeks' time that there were eviction proceedings under way for 5C, on whose button was written only the word *Shy*.

Were these mysterious facts intended to entice me, over lunch, into the writing of an afterword? It is true that in the following days, in the midst of a stalled book of my own, I began poking around on the web a bit.

I could and did find traces of Reginald Morse, of his essence— when I was willing to surrender the middle name, that is. He couldn't have been the R. E. Morse of Biloxi, Mississippi, for example, who had died in a hurricane-related traffic mishap in 1999 after racking up gambling debts. His family was interviewed on their front lawn, on the local news, the night of the tragedy, video footage available on YouTube. Weepy and regretful, they forgave him everything. With the Biloxi Morse out of the way, I tried a few other middle initials online, just to see if any led to the author of these reviews.

There was an R. L. Morse in Fairfax, Virginia, and astute readers of Morse's writings will note that on one occasion Reg Morse did in fact visit a hotel in Fairfax (see pp. 87–91). This R. L. Morse of Fairfax is a lawyer in private practice whose main line of business is real estate closings. I corresponded with R. L. Morse by e-mail a couple of times, and he seemed tickled by the possibility that he was a furious and infamous hotel reviewer, and if he was putting me on, he did a very good job of it. R. L. Morse explained, in the most genial way, that he didn't much like to travel.

There is a Reginald Edmund Morse of Tuscaloosa who works for the State of Alabama in child protective services. I had a hard time reconciling the number of weeks that this Morse, who goes by Reggie, gets off each year (ten business days) with the R. E. Morse who was constantly on the move, whose permanent address is a matter of debate.

R. G. Morse of Darien, Connecticut, comes from a long line of Morses, a family who manufactured candles in the state of Massachusetts over the course of centuries. R.G., the scion of the candle-making (and now air-conditioning) fortune, is in his early sixties and is suffering from metastatic prostate cancer, about which he is reasonably cheerful, an accomplishment, under the circumstances. Interestingly, R.G. told me that he is a keen student of famous hoaxes, for example the Ern Malley affair of the early twentieth century. According to R. G. Morse, Ern Malley was a modernist poet created one afternoon by two embittered pre-modernists (in Australia) in order to embarrass the editor of an Australian avant-garde periodical called *Angry Penguins.* Morse went on to allude to a number of other prominent literary hoaxes, including such celebrated imaginary writers as Wanda Tinasky, Adoré Floupette, and JT LeRoy, which led me to wonder if perhaps the Reginald Morse writings were the work of some prominent contemporary author in disguise. Talking to R. G. Morse didn't persuade me that he was involved with the work of our Reginald Morse (he said he was too ill to travel, and, if he were going to assume a pseudonym, would he really alter just the one initial?), but it did open up for me questions about fraudulence, about the relationship between the fraudulent and the genuine, and about the ways in which the fraudulent can sometimes feel closer to the truth than the supposedly genuine.

Last, I contacted an R. E. Morse in Canada, a person for whom this was not a legal name, as it turned out, but rather a pen name. R. E. Morse of Regina, Saskatchewan, was the author of numerous books about Canadian trees, plants, and birds (published mostly by the Modeste and Callahan imprint of Toronto), such as *Conifers of the Canadian Rockies*, *Coastal Ecosystems of Nova Scotia*, and *Tapping Your Own Sugar Maples!*, books often lavishly illustrated and dating back to the early seventies. The work of R. E. Morse (of Canada) is so historically bound, in terms of its look and feel, that it is hard to imagine this R. E. Morse having lived into the digital era at all. Moreover, this Canadian R. E. Morse was a woman. The possibility of gender imposture in the hotel reviews intrigued me, I'll admit, so I made a few inquiries among acquaintances, and these friends turned up the e-mail address of Ms. R. E. Morse, environmentalist and nonfiction writer. And so I did, at the risk of intruding, write to her:

Dear Ms. Morse,

Is it possible that you are the Reginald Edward Morse who wrote the popular online posts about North American hotels? I have been, as a sort of hobby, or perhaps as a bit of an obsession, chasing down the identity of this mysterious writer for some weeks, though I seem to be a long way from any definitive answer. Do you know anything about him? Any help you might provide in this regard would be most welcome.

My best wishes,
Rick Moody

Some weeks passed. Then, one Sunday, there was the familiar ping on my computer that indicated a new message, this one the most welcome reply from the writer I now understood to be a former prima ballerina, one of fewer than two hundred in the world so honored, Marina O'Shea, of Prince Edward Island, Canada:

Dear Mr. Moody,

I am most interested by your note, though unhappy to have to admit that I have no information regarding your Reginald Edward Morse. I do observe, however, Mr. Moody, that your own name sounds a bit like a pseudonym. I will tell you, in an indecorously self-involved way, that when I stopped professionally dancing, after a hip injury, and had to do something with my life, I chose the natural world for the locus of my writing because it was less taxing than the world of my dancer friends. Plants yielded to study and admiration without complaint. I enjoyed their company for decades, though I am now slowing down somewhat. I wrote to make some money, and I traveled a great deal, and that is the only aspect of my life that seems akin to your R. E. Morse. I am always glad to make the acquaintance of another writer, however, and especially one with whom I share some common interests. That said, I have never been to Tulsa. Nor Cleveland, though it's not far from Toronto. Perhaps you will be wondering how I chose such a tragicomic pen name, and in my case it had to do with a lover I once had who said that my birth name, Marina Orla O'Shea, sounded a bit like the word "morose."

With all best wishes,
R. E. Morse

Ms. O'Shea and I wrote back and forth for a while, at least when there was something newsy to discuss, and on one occasion Marina sent me a few haikus about her favorite Canadian broadleaf trees, such as the white mulberry. Then, three or four months after we had commenced our correspondence, Marina died rather suddenly. I was left with that acute sense of loss that you can have only when your friendship with someone is still in the planning stages. You see, I had confided in Marina O'Shea, as I had in no one else, about the extent of my Reginald Morse problem, which was that even though I hadn't even agreed to write this afterword yet, I was already expending more time on investigating Morse's identity than I was on my own work, without as yet having learned anything substantial at all.

Marina O'Shea, for her part, had more than a few things to say about Reginald Morse. I had sent this manuscript to Marina, and it was her contention that Morse, like Cervantes, was missing a hand or was otherwise seriously disabled, because, as she noticed, there were few, if any, descriptions of Morse's hands in his reviews, and when the little elegies about Morse's daughter appeared in the book, there were no descriptions of throwing this child up into the air. Marina observed—and surely here she was speaking from the vantage point of a lifetime of balletic experiences—that bearing a daughter aloft is one of life's most important pastimes, and sometimes fathers will throw a daughter into the air simply to try to restore themselves to spiritual equilibrium. And so unless Morse was missing a hand, Marina felt, or was otherwise disabled, there was not a chance that he had failed to engage in this curative activity.

Before I could write back to take issue with her theory, however, Marina abruptly ceased to be, following an aneurysm that spun itself into a coma (from which she did not awake), and her nephew, who made contact with some of her many correspondents, later wrote me to ask if I wanted some portion of her library. It turned out she owned a great number of books.

With Marina's death, it became clear that my need to know more about the specific biography of Reginald Edward Morse would ultimately be frustrated. I had exhausted most of my leads. Perhaps Reginald Morse, the fellow who wrote these lines, didn't want to be located, didn't want to be more than the posts you have read, and his need to conceal his physical self is a set of instructions about how the work is to be consumed, namely, that it is meant to be read for what it has to say about the world, not for what it has to say about Reginald Edward Morse. Maybe it would be useful to let Morse go, to follow the words instead. After all, men will let us down, but the work is fixed on the page.

In pursuit of the meaning of Morse's posts, I determined that in order to understand the associative breadth and the improvisatory immediacy of this literary work, I should experience some of the hotels Morse wrote about. I should try to know hotel life the way Morse knew it. I will add, in a spirit of full disclosure, that I personally like really good hotels. Prior to undertaking this assignment as the writer of the afterword to R. E. Morse's work, I had stayed in exactly two of the hotels in this book—the Plaza Hotel (of New York City) and the Hotel Whitcomb (of San Francisco). It is not so often, these days, that I get to stay in a hotel. When I do, I favor availing myself of what Morse refers to as amenities. I like to get a massage at a hotel; I like to get room service; and I will rifle a minibar for every last candy bar contained within. I do not refuse turn-down service. There really is nothing like having someone walk into your room in the evening hours to leave a foil-wrapped mint on your pillow.

Given that I have these feelings about hotel life—that hotel life should be a pampering experience—it was hard to get up my courage to stay in the Presidents' City Inn of Quincy, Massachusetts, one of the worst-rated hotels in the collected writings of Reginald Morse. (And this is as good a place as any to note that there is a great density of two-star ratings among Morse's reviews. So many that I had thought, at one time, that the publisher really ought to have entitled this book ★★, or perhaps ★★1/2. Furthermore, with the elusiveness of Reginald Morse in mind, it seems important to note that, as Michelle Perry told me, the legal department of the North American Society of Hoteliers and Innkeepers insisted on the inclusion of the words *a novel* on this work.) It happened that I was teaching for a week at the Lexington Academy, a secondary school in Lexington, Massachusetts. I had a very good time teaching at Lexington, which was a revelation, because my own teenage years at secondary school were characterized by emotional distress. The modern boarding-school student is better equipped than I was, more patient, more ambitious. I would go so far as to say that I enjoyed Lexington. The teaching paid well, and the school was covering my lodging. They were therefore understandably confused when I elected to stay at the Presidents' City Inn of Quincy, which is after all a known drug location. I claimed that I felt passionately about saving the school a little money and that I couldn't bring myself to stick them with a bill from the Ritz.

Unsurprisingly, I had a bad night at the Presidents' City Inn. First, my guitar, stored in the trunk of my BMW, was stolen. The trunk was wrenched open, and the guitar removed. It was my travel guitar and not of tremendous value, but it was stolen nonetheless. Meanwhile, the sound of monotonous computerized drumming from sport-utility vehicles with tinted windows was almost constant on the block in Quincy. As a result, I was more worried about getting caught in gang-related crossfire than I was about getting my guitar back. I had to call and text my wife repeatedly to tell her that I was still okay. I did not stay past the first night. There was a Courtyard by Marriott not far from the school.

So I can verify that the Presidents' City Inn is, indeed, a wreck of an establishment, and it's a miracle that there are paying clients who are willing, like the fly alighting on the transverse of the spiderweb, to put their cars in P in that parking lot and walk over to the bunker where one registers. Morse did so, and got one of his darkest reviews out of it. I didn't feel that the experience of staying there made me want to write, but I did feel, oddly enough, the emanations of Morse's prose style. This was a place he had been, after all, this man who receded from his own work like radiation from the blast site, and I knew, at this address, exactly how he had passed his night. I could have gone on and stayed at a few of the choicer residences described in these pages, like the Emerald Campsites, or the Norse Motel, or the bed-and-breakfast that is last in this sequence, but I would have learned only what is obvious, that this is not a book about hotels but a collection of writings about what it means to be alone.

The context of the work is crucial too, by which I mean its *online* publication, the contemporary world of the fast, cheap, and out of control. Despite Morse's brief infamy in that world, he's not even at the top of the comments section anymore. He's down in the archive now, deep in the space of the digital, in that sequence of nothings and somethings, a ghost inside a ghost of a machine. We like him, ultimately, because he's like us, but also not like us. He's a shadow, an imago, an ephemeral avatar of a human being, a voice in the wilderness whose work will never be troubled by an actual author appearing on daytime television. Morse is fragmentary, in that the pieces he wrote are themselves fragmentary, episodic, nonlinear, ending with new love simply because that is where he stopped.

That said, there's a danger in saying that this work is about only solitude and loneliness and the tendency of modern contrivances to aggravate our feelings of separateness. Maybe in the end I see in these pages exactly what I want to see, and maybe Reginald Morse has some other perfectly good reason for giving up reviewing and vanishing. Maybe Morse has taken a job as a motivational speaker at a college or university in the middle of the country and is better paid and no longer needs to write hotel reviews. Maybe his lover, K., has become his wife, and they have a new child, and he no longer has time to write these little screeds. Maybe he simply doesn't wish to travel anymore. Maybe he is tending to his aged mother, or maybe he has taken up gardening, has humus beneath his fingernails, and his daily life is now the antithesis of everything hip and Internet-related. We do not know. Our insistence on knowing is the limit of what we know about ourselves.

It's funny that I bring up K., because having put so much work into thinking about Reginald Morse, having been nudged into accepting the three-hundred-dollar fee for writing this afterword, and having written the lines above and determined that they were sufficient for this assignment, I visited an art opening one night, not too long ago, in Chelsea. There I met a woman who said her name was Leda, which, you probably know, is the name of a mythological character.

But let me back up for a moment. The curious fact is that at this particular opening, there was no work at all on the gallery walls. The space was entirely empty, and instead of a show, you were given, upon entering, a handout festooned in some kind of gold-leaf material, like a particularly garish wedding invitation, which explained that the artist had not been able, because of the abundant demands of a busy life, to make the work in question. We the audience simply had to imagine the art that might have been there, displayed upon these newly whitewashed surfaces. In the old conceptual-art days, they might have left out for us some art-making material—some crayons and scissors, some egg tempera or oils—and we the audience could have made the work, which the artist could then have sold as a hybrid artifact, a complex collaboration with the audience. But in this instance there was no work at all. We were therefore invited to imagine. Naturally, there was even more chatter than at a conventional art-world event. A great many people stared at the walls, mumbled to themselves, and shushed those who were overly involved with gossiping and drinking the white wine from the plastic stemware. A few sour intellectual types muttered into their personal digital devices. Perhaps they were uploading their reviews online.

In one corner, I snuck between a woman gazing at the wall and the wall itself, in that dance one does, and I felt awkward about my intrusion, exactly as though the wall did have work on it and not just the imaginary projections of concept. The woman laughed as if she knew what I was thinking, and we began talking, and she asked if I was an artist, and when I said that I was actually a writer, she said, *Oh, the form that features the least conceptual thinking.* She laughed again her slightly forced social laugh, weary and sympathetic and embarrassed all at once, and I didn't quite know what to make of her comment, and so I said something about the conceptual artist who had hung the blank canvas at which he had looked for a thousand hours. Somehow that analogy took us off on a tangent, conceptual-art pieces since the Fluxus movement, labor and fraudulence teetering in carefully balanced supply, which reminded me of the various novels that deal with this subject, novels of the confidence man, the grifter, the literary serial killer, et al., and that of course caused me to cite the work of Reginald Edward Morse. I had turned up no real traces of Morse, I explained to the woman who had introduced herself as Leda. She asked why I didn't go search for him in person, and I explained that others had already done so, with no success. It seemed there was no Reginald Edward Morse except the one in the work. She smiled a particularly enigmatic smile, and it was at this moment that I became convinced, abruptly and for no apparent reason at all, that Leda was K. herself. The erstwhile lover of Reginald Morse, the borrower of bird names, the muse and inspiration and co-agitator with Reginald Morse.

I had a sort of uncanny paroxysm in which the hair on my arms stood up for a second, and I shuddered. It was as if I had become the quarry of Reginald Morse, rather than the other way around, as if literature in general, and the online review in particular, always led to an electrical circuit of mystery and failure and repetition. I thought about this as I examined Leda's shoes, her rather scuffed-up flats (and this is to neglect to describe her face, which was long and sad, just this side of middle-aged, with bright red lipstick and somewhat pale skin, with blue eyes of the luminous slate-colored variety), and then I glanced up and said, *You wouldn't perhaps be a friend of Reginald Morse's, would you?*

Even as I asked, I was aware that the question would sound ridiculous, would sound as though I had lost my handhold on critical distance, and yet I went ahead and asked anyway, with the result that Leda became flustered and tried to excuse herself. With all the gentleness, even tenderness, that I could muster, I entreated, *Listen, I know, I know, this sounds crazy, and it probably has to do with how frustrated I already am because of this project. Forgive me. I didn't mean to make you uncomfortable. I'm the one who should be uncomfortable.* I touched her briefly, on the shoulder. She was wearing an off-white wool sweater that looked like it had been knitted in a Gaelic-speaking landscape. The touch was not intimate; it was a touch that was meant to signify earnestness. Or perhaps it meant that I understood our exchange was at an end. Which it was.

For a second, though, I had understood K., had seen into her and into her unlikely loyalty to Reginald Edward Morse. Maybe she was the portrait I would have painted on the blank walls of the gallery in Chelsea, or maybe she was the portrait that Morse would have painted, creating her likeness in a series of zeros and ones scratched with pen and ink. Whatever that blank space was, in that gallery, it was the space where imagination went, not the *thing itself,* in reality, but the subjective idea of the thing.

And that's how I feel about the writings of Reginald Edward Morse now, that they tell us more about the future than they tell us about hotels. I don't know if Morse's work is true, or genuine, or even if it's good, but I know that his work is a sign of the times, and that his laughter and his laments compose a novel in fragments in which the traces of a human pulsation are still audible at this distance, despite his silence. Maybe he's holed up in a motel by the interstate now, laughing at the bad customer service, like the jetliner that has gone radio silent but is still pinging from a distant satellite on its way to the bottom of the sea. Wherever he is, this future he suggests is scrawled in tragicomedy, and when you lay your hands on it, however accidentally, you feel the shadow of what's yet to come.

—*New York, May 2015*

- 27 December 1970 – 02 January 1971: **The Plaza Hotel, NYC, NY**
- 13 May 1984 – 14 May 1984: **Union Station, New London, CT**
- 24 June 1991 – 27 June 1991: **Emerald Campsites, Corinth, NY**
- 21 March 1996 – 22 March 1996: **Hampton Inn and Suites, Chicago, IL**
- 03 May 1997 – 04 May 1997: **Steamboat Inn, Mystic, CT**
- 05 January 1998 – 06 January 1998: **Groucho Club, London, UK**
- 01 July 2000 – 16 July 2000: **Masseria Salinola, Ostuni, Italia**
- 01 October 2001 – 03 October 2001: **The Equinox, Manchester, VT**
- 05 January 2002 – 09 January 2002: **La Quinta, Tusca loosa, AL**
- 05 May 2002 – 07 May 2002: **The Mercer Hotel, NYC, NY**
- 05 June 2002 – 12 June 2002: **Sand Trap Inn, Cannon Beach, OR**
- 21 November 2002 – 24 November 2002: **Americas [sic] Best Value Inn, Maumee, OH**
- 03 December 2002 – 05 December 2002: **Windmere Residence, Charlottesville, VA**
- 20 May 2004 – 22 May 2004: **Hotel Francesco, Roma, Italia**
- 03 June 2005 – 05 June 2005: **Mason Inn Conference Center and Hotel, Fairfax, VA**
- 02 March 2008 – 04 March 2008: **Presidents' City Inn, Quincy, MA**
- 08 October 2008 – 10 October 2008: **Sid's Hardware, Brooklyn, NY**
- 30 November 2009 – 01 December 2009: **Tall Corn Motel, Des Moines, IA**
- 06 December 2009 – 11 December 2009: **Norse Motel, Story City, IA**